HIS FINGERS T
caress the back of r
settled on my hip. ".
he whispered. "A glistening jev ... ... uarkness."

I blinked at him. "You say the strangest things to me."

"And I've only gotten started, sweetheart." His mouth settled over mine so quickly that I didn't understand what he was doing until his tongue parted my lips.

The world froze around me.

Because that brush of his mouth in the hallway before was nothing compared to *this*. He kissed me as if his life depended on mine to survive. I couldn't breathe beneath the intensity, the *ownership* of his touch.

Some part of me knew to fight.

While the other part sighed at the rightness of his caress.

I'm going insane.

I shouldn't be embracing him, yet I was. Vigorously, too. I even had my fingers in his hair. My damn body taking charge without my mind's permission. But I was too wrapped up in his touch to stop it, everything and everyone lost to the white noise of my thoughts.

His tongue moved against mine with the same skill he'd used to guide me around the dance floor, hypnotizing me into submitting.

A loud ding sent a jolt down my spine, drawing me back to reality like a slap across my face. It came from a clock somewhere in the ballroom, announcing the time. *Midnight.*

My eyes slid open to find a circle around us.

Just like that night freshman year.

Dread pooled in my belly.

A foreboding sensation crawling across my skin.

Tray smiled at someone over my shoulder, and my heart stopped. *Three, two...*

"Well, this looks cozy," Ryan said from behind me. "I barely even recognized you, Cindersoot. What with the makeover and all."

MIDNIGHT FAE ACADEMY

ELLA'S MASQUERADE: A PREQUEL

ELLA'S
MASQUERADE

A Midnight Fae Academy Prequel

USA Today Bestselling Author

Lexi C. Foss

This is a work of fiction. Names, characters, places, and incidents are either the product of the author's imagination or are used fictitiously, and any resemblance to actual persons, living or dead, business establishments, events, or locales is entirely coincidental.

Ella's Masquerade

Editing by: Outthink Editing, LLC

Proofreading by: Barb Jack

Cover Design: Jessica Allain, Enchanting Covers

Published by: Ninja Newt Publishing, LLC

Print Edition

ISBN: 978-1-950694-40-2

To Alyssa, for letting my muse spew nonsense at you daily—Ella's Masquerade was created as a result. You're an amazing friend, and I'm so glad angels brought us together. I'd be lost in this industry without you!

ELLA'S MASQUERADE

A MIDNIGHT FAE ACADEMY PREQUEL

PROLOGUE

ELLA

Freshman Year

LAUGHTER.

Jeers.

Cruel words.

It all blended around me, but certain voices peaked above the crowd.

"I can't believe she thought Dash actually wanted to go to the dance with her." Carmen's giggle followed, the sound grating on my nerves. My stepsister often woke me with that noise, usually before acting on whatever nefarious activity she and Ryan had plotted together.

"Classic Cindersoot, always living in her little dream world instead of our reality," Ryan said now, her cackle holding a sinister touch to it. I had no doubt this latest scheme was her idea. She was the more intelligent of the twin brats.

And somehow, they'd recruited Darlington Academy's very own prince to play in their twisted game.

I swallowed, the pain of their joint betrayal making it hard to breathe. As if I hadn't gone through enough this year. But that was exactly what Dash Charming had preyed upon. He was the one I'd confided in and cried to after my father's death.

Dash had just been so convincing.

After weeks of courting me, kissing me, holding my hand in the academy halls, telling everyone he *adored* me, I actually thought he liked me.

What was worse than falling for it was falling for *him*.

His wicked grin now told me it was all a lie.

A savage joke with me as the punch line.

And everyone knew.

What had he said about me behind my back? What had he told the others? Did he tell them all about my nightmares? About the shadows?

I shivered.

I always knew deep down something wasn't right. I'd just ignored my inner misgivings and given in to the fairy tale of reality. One my mother always told me existed. But her death had proven otherwise.

And then my father's passing this year...

I hung my head, my throat tight with emotion.

The entire freshman class stood around me, most of them amused. Some cast pitying glances my way, which was somehow worse.

Here I stood in my ruined blue gown, soiled by the punch Ryan had poured over my head. My blonde curls had absorbed the brunt of it, but my entire outfit was destroyed. Even my cerulean slippers.

My heart ached. No one could know what this night had meant to me. I'd dug the old dress out of the attic from my mother's former wardrobe and hemmed it myself to make it fit. Only to have it all so spectacularly spoiled.

I'm sorry, I whispered to her. *I'm so incredibly sorry.*

I knew better than this. All those who attended this academy were rich, elitist assholes who only thought of themselves. I was the one who didn't belong—the poor daughter taken in by her father's widow.

I'd begged my stepmother, Clarissa, to send me to the local high school. But she said I needed the academy, that it would set me up for the future.

Was this the future she had in mind?

Four years of hell?

"Oh, I think she's going to cry," Ryan mock-whispered.

Dash chuckled. "Should I offer a pity fuck?"

"She did look hot in that dress," his best friend drawled. "Bet she's a virgin, too."

Gross, I thought. We were only fifteen. Why wouldn't I be a virgin?

"Of course she is. No one in their right mind would ever touch her," Ryan replied, sounding far superior despite being a month younger than me.

Why am I still standing here? Because my feet had forgotten how to move. Well, they quickly remembered now. I refused to cry in front of them. Refused to let them see another moment of my agony.

I picked up my skirts and ran, their uproarious laughter trailing in my wake.

They'll all pay, I vowed. *One day, somehow they*—

A sob threatened my throat, cutting off my thoughts. I could plot my revenge later. Escaping mattered more.

Doors seemed to open for me, allowing me to burst into the night where all the cars waited.

I sprinted by them all, not caring in the slightest about the damp, snowy ground. The upcoming holidays were going to be hard—my first ones spent truly alone.

But this? The Freshman Holiday Ball? Had made it even worse. Because I had no one to run to.

No family.

No friends.

Not even a pet.

Tears trickled down my face, freezing in the night air. But onward I pushed, longing to leave everything behind me.

I had a month to pull myself together, to harden my shell, to not let their comments and cruelty impact me. I could do this. I had to.

Three and a half years. I could survive that. In three and a half years, I would be done with school, done with *them*.

My stepmother couldn't access my inheritance. Neither could I. Not until I graduated.

But on that very day, I would withdraw every penny and run far, far away.

Once I graduated, I would be free to—

My slippers gave out beneath me, sending me careening into a nearby wall. A wall with hands that grasped my hips to keep me upright.

I shook my head, clearing it and seeing the darkness around me for the first time. I'd run with a single-minded purpose of escape without paying any mind to my surroundings.

"Are you all right?" a deep voice asked, his face shrouded in the shadows. All I could make out were his piercing black eyes.

A chill swept up my spine. Something about this male was dangerous. It seemed to cloak his aura, allowing him to blend right into the night.

Or maybe it was my imagination.

Hell if I knew.

I took a step back, only to find myself caught in his too-strong grip. "Let go of me," I breathed, the demand in my tone hidden somewhere beneath my fraying emotions.

He released me in an instant, causing me to fall flat on my ass in a pile of dirty snow from the road. Of course. I wanted to scream at the unfairness of it all, to whimper at the cold, and to beat some sense into my guardian angel. Assuming she even existed. I was seriously starting to doubt any aspect of the universe cared about me at all.

The stranger's hand appeared, but I batted it away, too irritated to accept his help after being so unceremoniously dumped on the ground. A consequence that I recognized was more my fault than his.

I shoved myself upright, slipping again and landing against a real wall this time. With a determined growl, I took off again—in the right direction toward my home.

Home, I scoffed. *What is that anyway?*

"Hey!" the male called out behind me.

I ignored him.

This was the night from hell, and I just wanted it to end. My entire body was frozen, shivering, and probably dying from the wintry mix.

Wouldn't that be a grand finale to it all?

I wiped at the icy streaks against my cheeks, pushing myself onward. It wasn't until I reached the back entrance to my house that I realized why I was so cold.

I'd lost my slippers.

My *mother's* slippers.

I collapsed into a heap on the stoop, done with it all, and finally allowed myself to truly cry.

My fairy-tale evening had turned into a happily *never* after.

Because there was no such thing as love or joy in my world. Only harsh realities and cruel games.

And I was done being the butt of everyone else's jokes.

CHAPTER ONE

🌹 ELLA 🌹

Senior Year

SCHOOL UNIFORMS WERE THE BANE of my existence. What I wouldn't give for a damn hoodie to hide under.

Today's gossip surrounded some new kid. A transfer who had to shack up with his rich uncle for unknown reasons. Of course, the student population at Darlington Academy had several theories to discuss.

"I heard he was kicked out of his last school for lighting a teacher on fire."

"Meghan told me it was because his dad is in jail for embezzling money. So now he's, like, in hiding or something, with some super-pissed-off people after him."

"Pretty sure it's not that. I mean, did you see his car?

Can't buy that limited edition without funds, Cas."

"Tommy said he's the son of some mafia boss."

"Hmm, Tommy would know."

"Right?"

I rolled my eyes, pushing through the masses to get to my English class. These idiots seriously had too much time on their hands. It wasn't even first period, and they already had a hoard of backstories crafted for the new guy. Poor fool. He had no idea what kind of hellhole he'd just entered.

Eight more months, I told myself. *Then you're free.*

Technically, I was already eighteen and could leave now—something my stepmother enjoyed reminding me of every time she told me to earn my keep.

Alas, I required a degree to access my inheritance.

A stipulation my mother had put in the will.

And I couldn't exactly enroll myself in a public school without an address to call home.

So I was stuck in this hell until June.

The price we pay for a future, I thought with a snort, taking my usual seat at the back of the room.

I preferred to hide and take notes, which was easier back here away from the other students. Of course, that didn't stop them from harassing me.

With a sigh, I glanced up at the shadow approaching me. "Yes?" I said by way of greeting.

Charlie Anderson smirked, his too-perfect blond hair slicked back to reveal his classically handsome features.

All the girls adored him—the perpetual playboy and best friend to Dash Charming. The duo pretty much ruled the school, their families wealthier than God himself.

"Now is that any way to greet a prince, Cindersoot?" he drawled, propping his hip against my table.

"Oh, I'm sorry." I batted my eyes up at him. "Yes, Your Dickishness? How can I amuse you and your asshole friends today?"

He reached out to tug on one of the blonde strands of hair that had fallen out of my bun. I allowed it simply because I learned years ago that fighting back only earned me worse punishments. A lack of reaction, however, usually made them go away.

But not today.

No, the Royal Dick of Darlington Academy wanted something.

And he would toy with me until he got it.

Students began to enter, his back to them all as he considered my blouse and skirt. "Those look a bit big, Cindersoot."

"Because they are," I replied sweetly. "It used to belong to Ryan." The bitchy princess couldn't wear an outfit more than five times, despite it being a fucking uniform. And so I often inherited her hand-me-downs. Which would be fine if we had similar proportions. But she was all curves, while I had my mother's slender figure.

"A shame," he drawled. "I'd love to see more of the figure beneath."

I rolled my eyes. "Sure. How about later tonight?"

His lips curled. "Now you're speaking my language."

I matched his grin with one of my own. "Never going to happen, Sir Dickenstein." I blew him a kiss.

"We both know it would if I actually wanted it to," he replied, completely unfazed. "But no one wants to touch unwashed goods." He released my hair and wiped his hand on his pressed pants. "Try showering in the morning. I hear that helps."

I had showered this morning.

Then my stepmother had assigned me a last-minute task before school, which left me no time to wash up afterward.

Hence the foliage in my hair.

While I adored the autumn colors, I hated the chores that came with it. Because heaven forbid we have leaves in our yard. Why my stepmother bothered to keep all the trees on our property was beyond me. She clearly disliked them and the wildlife they brought into the yard.

He picked a leaf out of my hair and threw it in my face.

"You're filthy." He tsked. "Pretty sure that goes against the dress code."

I snorted, eyeing the display of tanned skin at his neckline. "So does not wearing a tie."

"I put it to a better use," he murmured, innuendo deep in his tone. "Not that I'd expect you to know anything about it." He leaned in close. "But maybe I'll demonstrate on you sometime. Deflowering virgins can be fun."

I canted my head to the side. "You think you could?" I asked, feigning innocence. "Because I could use a good mentor." I pretended to consider him. "Hmm, no, sorry. Chuckie Cheesy just isn't my style."

He narrowed his gaze, his playfulness slipping behind the callous mask I knew so well. "You're all about the nicknames today, aren't you, *Isabella*?"

"Well, when the shoe fits," I replied, shrugging.

He gripped my chin, bringing his nose to mine.

My heart skipped a beat, his nearness souring my stomach.

I hated when they touched me.

But they did it often, treating me like a chew toy they could stomp beneath their boot. No one ever did anything about it. Not even when their grip bruised—such as it did now.

The administrators at this esteemed academy cared more about their budgets than their students. I was just a charity case, someone lucky to be here. It didn't matter that it was *my* father's money that paid the bills. No. He was dead, leaving Clarissa in charge of his estate.

"Careful, Cindersoot," Charlie warned, his lips falling to my ear. "Push me and I'll push back."

He released my chin to place his palm between my breasts and gave me a shove that sent my chair back a foot.

"You reek," he snapped, standing upright and sneering at me. "Stay back there. The rest of us value our sense of smell." With that, he turned and approached a horde of giggling girls and smirking guys.

Our audience.

Yeah, enjoy the show, I thought, scooting my chair loudly back to my seat.

Because fuck him and his command.

He either didn't hear me move or didn't care. Likely the latter. His bullying attempt for today was done, making him the center of attention. The king lording over his minions.

At least Dash wasn't in this class. Handling both princes of this kingdom created quite the headache.

Everyone fell silent, sending a chill down my spine.

Shit. He noticed and now—

"You must be the infamous Trayton Nacht," Charlie drawled, his shoulders tightening beneath his blazer jacket as he faced the front of the room.

"I'm not sure about *infamous*" was the reply. Goose bumps pebbled across my skin, the newcomer's voice deep and masculine with a slight lilt. "And I prefer Tray."

A glance around the room confirmed I wasn't the only female affected.

Gleams of interest came from the feminine population, while jealousy mingled with curiosity on the male faces. I couldn't see the new guy, but he clearly had a physical impact.

Which explained Charlie's defensive stance.

He didn't take kindly to men who threatened his position as the hottest guy in the school. Only Dash could share it with him.

Although, some would argue it was Charlie who actually shared the spot with Dash. Not the other way around.

Regardless, this new guy clearly provided some competition.

"Charlie Anderson," Darlington Academy's prince informed the newcomer. "Son of Jackson Anderson."

Silence.

After a long beat, Tray said, "Oh, sorry. Was that supposed to mean something to me?"

My lips quirked up. *Wrong thing to say, buddy.* But

admirable at the same time.

"Owner of Anderson Motors," Charlie replied, folding his arms. His back was still to me, blocking my view of the new guy. But I could sense the tension rising between them.

"Yeah, sorry, I'm not familiar with the American automotive industry. But congratulations on the relation." He stepped around him, providing me with my first look at the guy who dared defy Darlington royalty.

Reddish-brown hair.

Square jaw.

Strong neck.

Lack of an understanding on how to properly wear the academy uniform—a leather jacket was not the same thing as a blazer.

He plopped down at the table in front of me, everything about his lazy sprawl saying how he felt about Charlie's little inquisition. "I do not give a fuck" was practically plastered to the dude's forehead.

Well, this would make things interesting.

How long would his little rebel act last against the princes of Darlington Academy?

I gave him a week before they recruited him into their circle. He had just the right amount of arrogance to qualify, and his looks certainly guaranteed him entrance to the female elite's bedrooms. This was all just a glorified interview to see how quickly he succumbed to their power. Once he did, he'd be given a status. And the rest would be history.

Professor Montgomery entered with a flourish, dispelling Charlie's chance to follow up with the new guy. "Be seated, be seated," she said, waving her arms around with the words. The woman always did have a flair for the dramatic. With her wiry white hair pulled back in a severe bun, she resembled a strict woman. But kindness lurked in her bright blue gaze.

I adored her and her crazy methods.

Such as now. She narrowed her gaze at Trayton Nacht

and snapped her fingers. "Well, on with your introduction, then."

Straight to the point, as always.

I smirked as he sat up a little straighter and cleared his throat.

Yeah, Montgomery doesn't play.

"Tray," he said.

And he didn't say anything else.

"Tray," she repeated after a beat. "This is an English class, Tray. We use full sentences. Now stand up and give a proper introduction."

"Sure." He pushed his chair away and stood, his height seeming to dwarf me beneath a shadow. Because yeah, he was handsome *and* tall.

Aren't they all? I thought with a mental scoff.

He glanced over his shoulder at me, his irises an exotic blend of obsidian and dark chocolate colors. My favorite kind of drink. Not that I wanted to taste him.

"My name is Trayton Nacht," he said, still looking at me. "I prefer to be called Tray." He turned back around, facing Professor Montgomery. "Was that sufficient enough? Or do I need to prepare a full biography?"

Several of the students snickered.

I bit my lip, knowing this would not go over well. At all.

Professor Montgomery's resulting smile confirmed my thoughts. "That is an excellent idea, Mr. Nacht." She clasped her hands, her eyes dancing around the class. "And as all of you are smiling, I can see you agree. We'll make this a group assignment, so everyone can participate."

The snickers turned to groans while I just shook my head.

Idiots.

"Peer interviews," Professor Montgomery continued. "With a three-to-five-page full-length biography due by Friday."

As it was Tuesday, that only gave us three days to complete the assignment.

Fan-fucking-tastic.

Tray reclaimed his seat, that lazy sprawl in full effect again. "My life isn't that interesting. How about a page instead?"

Professor Montgomery arched a brow. "Well, then I pity your partner because the requirement is three to five pages. And you will be writing the biography of the student you interview, not your own biography, Mr. Nacht."

More groaning from the class.

Tray, however, grinned. "Brilliant. Are we to choose our partners?"

Man, this guy didn't know when to quit. He'd be in detention by the end of the day if he kept up this pace.

I shook my head just as our professor declared, "No, I'll be choosing. And since Ms. Cinder seems to disapprove of this assignment, I'll be pairing you with her." She gave me a look that had me rolling my eyes.

That wasn't at all why she'd paired me with him.

She paired us because she knew I wouldn't let him cheat.

Rude. Looked like I needed to reevaluate my Favorite Teacher Award.

Montgomery began assigning everyone else partners for the project, the class growing reluctantly quiet. "You can all thank Mr. Nacht for giving me the idea," she added at the end, essentially hammering a nail into his social-status coffin.

Of course, he merely appeared amused by it all, his full lips tilted upward in a cocky grin. "You're welcome," he said.

Charlie cut him a glare.

Several others followed suit.

Hmm, maybe Trayton Nacht wouldn't be inducted into the royalty circle by the end of the week. Especially if he continued to piss everyone off.

Trina raised her hand from the front row, her perfect hair matching her perfectly pressed uniform. Professor Montgomery arched a brow, her signature way of calling upon a student. "Can we have the rest of today's class to work on our assignment?" she asked. "With this being Homecoming week, most of us are involved in mandatory activities after school. And the squad has extra practices as well."

"Not to mention football practice," Charlie drawled.

Ah, yes, the extracurriculars were always more important than the academics.

Which was exactly why Montgomery paused to consider the request.

"I will extend the assignment's due date to next Friday," she decided. "That should account for this week's plans, yes?"

Tray actually appeared surprised.

The rest of the class looked relieved.

"But the assignment is to be completed outside of school. I expect thorough interviews and a truthful biography as a result." She looked pointedly at the students who typically faked their way through this course. "No writing each other's essays. I'll know."

That would be the easy way out.

But I knew better than to try Montgomery's patience.

"In fact, I want at least two hours of logged time for the interviews, with thorough notes and visual proof that you met. That shouldn't be too hard for those of you who adore your camera phones." Her focus fell on Trina.

The blonde bundle of perfection simpered. "Of course, Professor Montgomery. That won't be a problem for most of us." She glanced at me with those words.

"I'll be fine," I drawled. "But thanks for your concern, Princess Perfect."

"Poor new kid has to deal with the leaf lover," Charlie added. "Sorry, buddy. I hope she at least showers before your interview date."

"That's enough, Mr. Anderson," Professor Montgomery snapped. She was the only one in this whole school who ever sort of stood up for me. It made me love her and despise her at the same time.

I didn't need a savior. I saved myself every damn day, thank you very much.

She dove into today's lecture with a flourish, not wanting to waste another second. Which she knew would happen if she allowed me to speak up for myself. I had no problem putting Charlie Anderson in his place.

Tray tilted his chair to place his back to the wall, his sideways sprawl on his chair allowing him to see me and the front of the room at the same time.

I pretended not to notice him.

Not even when he looked directly at me.

Which, yeah, was awfully distracting. The male had a presence about him that just seemed to consume the room. And his attitude told me he knew it, too.

Definitely cocky with a hint of rebel underneath. Hence, the leather jacket. Something I just realized Professor Montgomery hadn't commented on.

Strange.

She was usually a stickler for the dress code, having just—

"You don't care for showers?" he asked softly, his voice pitched too low for anyone else to hear.

I blinked at him, startled by the mental interruption.

"Fascinating," he added with a subtle sniff of the air. "You smell delicious to me."

My eyes widened. "Excuse me?" I matched his pitch, not wanting to call attention to myself. The professor would not take kindly to us whispering during her lecture.

Tray opened his bag, pulled out a piece of paper, and doodled on it before sliding me the note. "Here's my number. For our assignment."

"I don't have a phone," I replied, passing it back. "We'll need to meet through other means."

His brow drew downward. "Who doesn't have a phone in this century?"

"Me." Because my stepmother insisted I didn't need one.

"Is there something the two of you would like to share with the class?" Professor Montgomery demanded.

"Nothing important, just asking her if she needed to borrow some soap," Tray drawled. Which earned a snicker from Charlie and a glower from me. "You know, to help with the showering problem."

Professor Montgomery turned an uncomplimentary shade of red. "I realize this is your first day, Mr. Nacht, but I will not tolerate bullying or disruptive behavior in this class. One more outburst or unruly comment will leave me no choice but to send you to the headmaster. Am I clear?"

"I thought I was being helpful," he replied, lifting his hands in surrender. "Feedback duly noted."

My head hit the desk. *Imbecile.*

And Professor Montgomery snarled. "Headmaster Jeffries's office. Now."

"I'll need someone to give me directions," he said, collecting his stuff into a bag and standing.

"Ms. Cinder," the professor said through her teeth. "Please escort our new student to Headmaster Jeffries. Perhaps it will give you both time along the way to arrange your future interviews."

Why the hell am I looped into this jackhole's punishment? I wondered, flabbergasted. "Seriously?" I said out loud, lifting my head.

"Seriously," she snapped.

I clenched my jaw and grabbed my stuff. As if I would ever leave it alone for Charlie or his minions to mess with.

"Fine." I pulled the strap over my shoulder. "You." I hit him with my best glare. "Follow." I didn't wait for his agreement, my tone already implying I wouldn't accept anything less than obedience.

I stomped toward the door, ignoring the professor along the way. Because yeah, I'd definitely be reevaluating my "favorites" system after this.

Tray woofed at my back, pretending to be a dog and eliciting a round of laughs from the class.

I lifted my eyes to the ceiling in response.

This guy was just like the rest of them—an immature jackass with too much time and money on his hands.

Eight months, I told myself. *Eight. More. Months.*

Then I would be free of this hellhole and would never have to look back.

CHAPTER TWO

MMM, DELECTABLE, I thought as I followed Isabella Cinder down the empty corridor of Darlington Academy.

She'd grown up since our first meeting in that alley just under three years ago. As had I. If she recognized me now, she didn't show it. She'd left me in such a hurry, her sodden slippers a pale blue lump in the dirty street snow.

I wouldn't allow her to escape again.

No. I'd come here specifically for her. There were things she didn't understand, and the Council had tasked me with explaining them to her. Well, more like I'd offered. It had been me who found her, after all.

They all agreed to wait until she turned eighteen before recruiting her into our world.

Well, the time had come.

The poor little darling had no idea who her parents really were or the destiny they'd dropped into her lap. She would soon. After we finished a few games first.

"Here," she said, stopping abruptly at the administrative office. "Have fun."

My palm hit the wall, blocking her exit. "You're not going to escort me inside?"

Gorgeous blue eyes narrowed up at me, the color reminding me of the dress she wore the night we first met. "I'm pretty sure you'll be fine on your own."

"Maybe I'm shy."

She snorted. "Yeah, I believe that." She folded her arms, sassy energy flaring all around her. When she grew into her powers, she'd be a force of nature. I couldn't fucking wait. "I can only meet for an hour after school each day for our project. So pick two days for our interview and we'll get it over with as soon as possible."

"Oh, I already picked a day."

She waited.

I didn't elaborate, just continued to stare her down with my arm caging her in. She could have stepped back to escape, but the feisty female remained steady before me, totally unfazed by my nearness.

So very different from the women at Midnight Fae Academy. Cornering one of them in this manner would have led to seduction and sensual fun—the benefits of being a royal.

But Isabella didn't seem to notice my natural charms at all. If anything, she appeared completely uninterested.

Fascinating.

"And which day would that be?" she prompted, her patience thinning.

I smiled. "Saturday."

Her brow furrowed. "I meant a weekday. After school. Unless you plan to attend class on Saturdays?"

"No, I plan to go to Homecoming. With you as my date." I leaned into her, adoring the way her slender form seemed to fit against my much taller one. "Try to wear something nice, Ms. Cinder." I picked one of the sticks from her bun and let it fall to the floor between us. "I'll pick you up at six. We'll interview each other over dinner before the dance."

I pressed my lips to her cheek and stepped around her as she sputtered something unintelligible at my back.

"What?! You—"

I disappeared into the administrative office before she could finish. The delicious female could reject me all she wanted, but by Saturday, she'd accept. Because, by then, she'd know why I was here. At least part of the reason. And she'd be too intrigued to resist.

Welcome to my world, Isabella Cinder.
I do hope you want to stay and play for a while.
Because you're mine now, sweetheart.

CHAPTER THREE

❧ ELLA ❧

HOMECOMING.

He had to be joking.

Messing with me.

He didn't even know my name, for crying out loud. Well, he knew my last name. But taking me to a dance? Yeah, no, that wasn't happening. I didn't attend school functions, not since freshman year.

I shivered at the memory. *Not happening*. Nope. The joke was on the new guy. He could find someone else to toy with because I didn't indulge in these games. Not with him. Not with anyone.

Oh, but he'd certainly made an impression on all the girls. He was the hot topic of the afternoon in the girls' locker room, despite having missed lunch. Many speculated that he'd ditched the rest of the day after his date with the headmaster this morning, but his car was still in the lot. Some of the others thought he might be loitering on academy grounds.

My opinion? Good riddance.

Closing my locker, I picked up my cap and goggles from the bench and made my way through the doors that led to the natatorium. All students were required to enroll in one physical course every year. I chose swimming because my stepsisters didn't know how, and it was fun to be able to do something they couldn't.

Unfortunately, Charlie and Dash were both swimmers.

Which meant they were in this class.

I ignored them as I always did and knelt to dip my cap in the water. Heat blanketed my exposed back when I stood, causing me to sigh. *Here we go,* I thought, very familiar with this game.

Charlie didn't even give me a chance to turn around before he nudged me hard in the hip, sending me into the water.

Or maybe it was Dash today.

Who the fuck knew?

I pushed off the bottom of the pool, but rather than shoot up in the lane I'd "fallen" into, I kicked to give myself some distance. I made the mistake once of trying to resurface in the same lane and found my hair trapped in a fist for far too long.

Never again.

I stole a breath and made for the next lane, just in case one of the idiots had tried to follow me, and started sprinting for one of the walls.

Fortunately, I beat them to the starting block and was able to hoist myself up onto the deck again.

Masculine laughs sounded from the edge. I ignored them in favor of putting on my cap, but as I slid my goggles on, I realized there were three guys, not two.

Trayton Nacht.

I narrowed my gaze. Was he the one who pushed me in? Because he appeared rather amused standing there in just a pair of swim trunks.

Several of the females were gaping openly at the rippled muscles lining his torso, as if they'd never seen an athletic male. Like, hello, Dash and Charlie maintained the same physique. All right, sure, Tray had the whole windswept-auburn-locks thing going for him, and those golden-flecked eyes. But he was built just like the other guys. It also seemed he was fitting in with their crowd already by the way they slapped him on the back as if congratulating him.

Why? Because he pushed me in? I wondered, pursing my lips. *Yes, let's all bond over picking on poor little Cindersoot.*

Whatever.

I'd drown all their asses in a race soon. It drove Charlie crazy that he couldn't catch me. Dash, however, frequently tied me. So how would Mr. Nacht do? He certainly had the body of a swimmer, with his broad shoulders, tapered waist, and long legs. A freestyler's build, if my swimmer's eye was right.

Hmm. This might get interesting because Dash also favored short-distance freestyle events.

"I see you finally took a shower, Cindersoot," Charlie drawled as the trio approached.

My lips curled as I slid my goggles over my eyes. "And I see you found yourself a new boyfriend, Chuckie. That's sweet." I blew them both a kiss and dove into the water before anyone could retaliate. Looked like I was starting my warm-up early, and from the splashes behind me, so were the guys.

Great.

They would be delayed by their own caps and goggles, giving me the chance to get a head start in the fifty-meter pool. Of course, on the way back, I'd have a problem. Maybe I'd hop out of the water and walk around.

Or—

A hand gripped my ankle, yanking me backward into a

hard body.

I squealed, my momentum no longer heading in the direction I desired.

Shit! I latched onto a pair of masculine shoulders, the water too deep for me to stand. This wasn't good. I needed to fight, to scratch my offender and get the hell out of Dodge.

Only, he didn't even flinch as my nails dug into his skin, instead grasping my hips and pulling me flush against him. "I'm not going to hurt you," he whispered against my ear.

I blinked, startled. "Tray?"

"Trust me," he breathed, his lips brushing my cheek just like they did earlier.

My eyebrows drew down. "I don't even know you."

"You're about to," he replied as the water around us shifted.

Dash reached us first, his triumphant gaze making my stomach twist. But it was Charlie's arrival and his vengeful glower that had me sweating, even in the water.

Three males, little old me, and a bunch of student spectators.

This could not end well.

Where's Grayson? I wondered, my eyes dancing around the pool for the swim coach. He usually drew up sets on the board for practice. Of course, he was nowhere to be seen. Meaning I had absolutely no backup here.

Tray's thumb brushed my hip bone, sending a shiver up my spine. Did he have to hold me so close? I could actually *feel* him through our swimsuits, his growing interest a brand against my lower belly. Not good. Not good at all.

And what business did he have being attracted to me?

"I see you caught a dead fish," Charlie said, his tone chilling the air.

"Oh, I don't know about dead," Tray mused, his grip tightening. "Feels pretty lively to me."

"Let me go," I demanded, my fingers clutching his upper arms.

"Nah, I like you right where you are, Isabella."

"Isabella?" I repeated. "No one calls—" I choked on a mouthful of water as he harshly jerked me under the surface, his palms cement blocks against my sides.

Male chuckles reverberated above, the sound distant to my ears. I clawed at Tray's stomach, demanding my release, but the jackass didn't even budge.

My legs scissored, creating a whirlpool beneath us as I fought for leverage.

Nothing.

Fuck!

My lungs began to burn, my energy expelled from trying to fight the brick wall that was Trayton Nacht.

I grabbed his swim trunks and tried to yank them down as a last resort.

The tie held.

He couldn't just drown me. But something about the way he held me had me second-guessing that assessment.

My limbs began to tingle.

My need to breathe taking over in a convulsion that had me opening my mouth.

And sweet air suddenly hit me in the face, causing me to gasp in agony.

Dash and Charlie were laughing hysterically.

But Tray's eyes were on mine, an intensity in them that had me blinking rapidly and sputtering liquid from my mouth. "Let's see you finish that lap now," he taunted, harshly shoving me away from him.

I didn't think, my arms and legs already moving as I fought the ache building inside my chest. A tidal wave rode my tail, the trio having taken off after me like some sort of screwed-up chase.

I dove under the lane lines, searching for the side of the pool, and forced myself out of the water before they could catch me. Every part of me trembled, from my head to my toes, the vivid sensation of drowning haunting each fresh inhale.

Tray reached the side first, but rather than jump up after me, he placed his arms on the edge and looked me over. Charlie and Dash weren't as casual, their anger palpable.

"What the fuck was that, man?" Charlie demanded.

Tray's lips curled briefly, and he winked at me before his features fell behind a cool mask. "What the fuck was what?" he asked, glancing at my tormentors. "The mouse got away. We'll chase her again soon."

"Because you used my torso as a fucking springboard," Charlie snapped, pulling himself out of the water.

And sure enough, he had a red mark forming on his abdomen.

That's interesting. I was almost jealous.

"My bad, man," Tray said, releasing the wall. "I was eager to play with my new toy."

My stomach churned. *I am not a fucking toy.*

"I don't know about the rest of you, but I'm ready to swim some laps. We'll catch up after." He released the wall and floated off on his back. After a few flutter kicks, he turned onto his stomach and took off toward the other end with long, strong strokes.

No wonder he'd caught me.

The dude was a freaking fish.

"This isn't over, Cindersoot," Charlie hissed, drawing my attention back to him.

"It never is," I muttered, forcing myself to stand on shaky legs. "But I've had enough for today."

With that weak retort, I headed to the one place they couldn't follow me—the girls' locker room.

CHAPTER FOUR

TRAY

MY BLOOD BOILED, magic flaring at my fingertips. It took physical restraint not to lash out at Charlie and his buddy Dash. Drowning them would have been too easy.

Also, I couldn't. They deserved to suffer for their crimes against Isabella. And she needed to be the one to make them pay for their years of torment.

However, the two females leaning up against my car now would serve as the grand finale.

Ryan and Carmen Cinder, the queen bees of Darlington Academy.

Short skirts, loosely buttoned blouses, and lips painted a shade of fuck-me red. They were the definition of trying too hard. Very unlike their gorgeous stepsister, who didn't need a smear of makeup to enhance her naturally beautiful features.

I hit the button to unlock my car, opened the passenger door, and tossed my bag inside. Ryan and Carmen remained against the driver's side, their matching brown eyes glimmering as I approached.

"Ladies," I greeted, forcing a smile. "Are you looking for a ride?" I'd prefer to drive them straight to hell, where they belonged, but that wasn't part of the game. If Isabella chose to send these bitches to a cruel fate, then so be it. For now, however, I had to play my part.

"We hear you're interested in our stepsister," Carmen said, her finger twirling a platinum blonde strand.

"Yeah?" I propped my hip against my car and slowly checked her out.

Plump breasts, tiny waist, long legs.

I could see the appeal to the human male population, but beneath her porcelain skin lived a witch with evil claws.

"Who's your stepsister?" I asked, pretending I didn't know anything about the infamous Cinder sisters. "Does she look anything like you?" That would be a straight no. Isabella's hair was a natural blonde shade, her body slender and lean but curved in all the right places, and she had a face I could study forever without growing bored.

It was why Dash and Charlie were obsessed with her. Oh, they used her sisters' penchant for bullying Isabella as an excuse for their actions, but both men wanted to fuck her. I could see it in their eyes today when she stepped onto the deck in that formfitting swimsuit. They bullied her because it gave them a reason to touch her.

Hence, my interference.

Which hadn't won me many points, but hell if I was going to sit there and watch them torment her.

Carmen giggled while Ryan laughed, drawing me back to this stupid exercise.

"Me? Look like Isabella?" Carmen sounded offended, which caused my lips to twitch. Because yeah, there was definitely no resemblance between the two. And Ryan wasn't any better with her fake nose and bleached white teeth.

Both these chicks were like an advertisement for airbrushing gone wrong.

"Trust me, only rodents resemble our wretched stepsister," Ryan put in, stepping toward me and running a blood-red nail down my chest. "But we're curious why you're interested in her."

"Yes, rumor has it you had some fun with her in the pool," Carmen added, also invading my personal space to grasp my arm.

Very forward.

Confident.

And clearly in the mood for control.

But these two had no idea whom they were propositioning.

I grabbed Ryan's hip and yanked her closer, loving the way she gasped at my abruptness. *Try to manipulate me,* I thought. *I dare you.*

"My interest is my business," I told her instead, catching her gaze and holding it. "But you've piqued mine, sweetheart. Shall I have some fun with you instead?"

Because lighting you on fire would be incredibly entertaining, I added, amused with the image that stirred in my head.

Her palm flattened against my chest, her body pressing into mine in a practiced way that bespoke of sexual experience.

Yet it did nothing for me. If anything, it took physical effort not to outwardly cringe.

"Mmm, I think I would enjoy that," she murmured, her lips falling to my ear. "However, I'll need proof that you're up to the task."

Carmen leaned into my opposite side, her fingers running through my hair. "Oh, I think he is, Ry," she said conversationally. "In fact, I think this could be a lot of fun."

"Are you suggesting a test, sis?" Ryan cooed.

"I am." She batted her eyes at me, moving even closer.

29

"A challenging one."

Ah, this was too easy. Only here a day and they were falling into my trap without any pushing on my part. Brilliant. "I'm listening," I murmured, tightening my grip on Ryan's hip. She was clearly the ringleader, so I focused on her. "What did you have in mind, sweets?"

"Poor Ella hasn't had a date to a dance in so long. I think you should ask her." She walked her red claws up and down my shirt, making me want to burn the offending digits with a sweep of power.

Fortunately, her words were music to my ears.

"You want me to take another woman—this *Ella*—to a dance?" I reiterated.

She nodded. "But not just that. I want you to humiliate her."

I frowned. "Why?"

Her shoulder lifted. "Because she's a conceited little tramp who thinks she's better than the rest of us."

"And no one has gotten her to a dance since freshman year," Carmen added.

"Still not seeing a benefit to this," I drawled, leaning in to draw my nose across Ryan's cheek. "You seem more my speed. How about I take you instead?"

Her laugh was one of those fake tinkling noises that made most men cringe. So over the top, just like the rest of her.

"Well, if you do your job right, you'll get both of us as a prize," Ryan taunted, glancing conspiratorially at her sister before narrowing her dull gaze at me. "But only if you make her cry, new guy. Like, embarrass her well and truly. We're talking full breakdown."

My eyebrows lifted. "And I get the two of you as a reward after?" Did men actually fall for this bullshit?

Oh, right. I'd met two idiots who did earlier.

Apparently, the whole twin-sister fetish in this realm really fucked with human morals.

Ryan nodded. "You get us both for as long as you want."

"However you want," Carmen said, taking on her role of seductive sidekick and pressing her ample breasts into my arm.

"That's an intriguing proposition, ladies," I admitted. *But not for the reasons you assume.*

Having them both in any position I wanted would be a dream come true. Because I'd tie them to a stake and burn them alive.

Man, how did Isabella live with these cunts?

"So what do you say, hotshot?" Ryan asked, her voice taking on a husky tone before brushing her lips over my jaw.

I say I need a shower, love, I thought, fighting off a gag and instead forcing my lips to curl. "It's going to take more than a dance to humiliate her to the point of a breakdown," I said, needing an excuse to have as much access to Isabella as possible. "We're talking months for what you're looking for, which means I'll be requiring more than one night between the two of you."

Intrigue flashed in Ryan's features. "It sounds like you have some experience in breaking a woman."

Now I really did smile, my hand sliding to the small of her back to splay against her spine. "You have no idea, sweetheart," I drawled against her ear and pulled back. "If you want my services, you're going to have to pay. Significantly."

The girls shared a look, devious energy practically breeding between them.

I had them right where I wanted them.

Not only would they provide me with every excuse to get closer to Isabella, but they would also thank me for it.

For every moment up until they learned the truth.

And their stepsister destroyed them.

Fucking beautiful. I couldn't wait.

"All right," Ryan murmured. "Convince Ella to attend Homecoming with you this weekend. Do that, and we'll know you're serious. Then we can talk about a price."

"Homecoming," I repeated, pretending to think it over.

Clearly, Isabella hadn't said a word to anyone about my proposition this morning. Not that I was surprised. She had no intention of joining me. But I'd change her mind soon enough.

"We'll give you a taste of what's to come Saturday night," Ryan added in an attempt to sweeten the deal. "Consider it a test both ways. We'll see if you're as good as you seem to think you are, and we'll prove we're better than you could ever dream."

I smirked. "I think you have that backward, dove." I tapped her on her nose. "Because I'm far better than you could ever dream."

"Then prove it," she taunted. "Take Ella to Homecoming."

"If I do, the game begins," I warned. "And I have to pretend to be hers, or there'll be no future play."

Respect gleamed in Ryan's irises. "Understood. We'll be discreet."

I nodded. "Then you have yourself a test play, sweets." My palm went to her hip again, squeezing. "Now tell me your names."

They both giggled, shaking their heads. "As if you don't know," Ryan said.

"I don't." A total lie, but I enjoyed seeing some of the light dim from their eyes.

"Really?" Carmen sounded shocked.

"First day, new guy, remember?" I released Ryan. "I don't even know who this Ella is yet."

"The girl you dunked in swim class," Carmen replied, her brow furrowing.

"Cinder?" I asked, snorting. "I thought this was supposed to be a challenge?"

Ryan laughed outright, shaking her head. "Oh, new guy, you have no idea. And I'm Ryan. This is Carmen. You'll know all about us by the end of the week, assuming you don't skip all your classes."

I feigned amusement. "You heard about my day, did

you?" I folded my arms to afford me some breathing room because their perfume was starting to give me a headache. Neither chick received the message.

"We hear everything at this school," Ryan said, her statement resembling a threat. "We own this school."

"Fascinating." And unfortunately true, from what I'd observed. "Well, it was lovely meeting you both, but I have a plot to conceive and only three days to make it happen. Unless you want to give me a taste of our deal now?"

Carmen seemed on board with the idea.

Ryan merely smiled. "Not a chance, new guy. Prove yourself first, then we'll talk."

I returned her amusement. "I'll more than prove myself." With a wink, I pulled open the door to my car, successfully dislodging them along the way. "I look forward to our future together, ladies. I think it'll be pleasurable indeed." *Particularly when I awaken Isabella's powers and watch her fry you both alive.*

Ah, and what a sight that would be.

"To the future," I said, sliding into my car and shutting the door. *May you both burn for eternity.*

CHAPTER FIVE

"WHAT THE HELL IS THIS?" I demanded, thrusting a document into Tray's face.

Not two minutes into my Wednesday morning and already I was in a mood. Courtesy of the new student jackass who had taken the table in front of mine in English again.

Just because we had a project to work on together did not mean we needed to sit near one another. I'd address that point just as soon as he explained the paper he'd left on my chair.

He barely looked at it, his eyebrow inching upward to his hairline. "A list of questions for our dinner Saturday." He folded his arms, his legs doing that man sprawl he seemed to prefer. Somehow it made him appear both lazy and elegant at the same time. "If you could put yours together for me to review by tomorrow, that'd be great. I want to make sure I'm prepared."

I sputtered, glancing at the words on the page and then back at him. "*These* are your interview questions?" I started reading them out loud. "Favorite date location. Favorite flower. Favorite dessert. Favorite place to be kissed." I shook my head. "This sounds like an online dating site, not a class assignment."

"Consider it a creative combination of activities." His lips curled, a pair of dimples creasing at the ends. "I can't wait to see your questions for me, Isabella. Feel free to request demonstrations as well."

My eyes narrowed. "Can you demonstrate stabbing yourself?"

"Sure," he replied, fisting his hand over his chest and giving it a good bump. "Does that work for you, darling?"

"With a knife would be even better."

He tsked. "There are so many more-intriguing ways to use a weapon." He pushed off his chair, his over-six-foot frame dwarfing my five-foot-five one. I fought to maintain my stance as he moved into my personal space, his palm landing on my hip. "Perhaps I'll bring a dagger Saturday to show you."

I narrowed my gaze up at him. "I already told you that I prefer a weekday."

"Which is just too bad because Saturday is my only offer." He slid his hand upward to my side, his touch a brand through my thin, academy-embroidered blouse. "Unless you want to fail our first assignment together?" he offered. "I would be happy to play the rebel card with you any day, darling."

"What do you have going on after school that makes you only available on the weekends?" I demanded.

"Yes, I like that question. Add it to your list." His hand moved to my lower back, pulling me forward into the warmth of his body. "But try to be creative with the other questions, Isabella. I intend for us to get to know one another. Intimately."

I hated the shiver that final word elicited.

Hated even more that I *liked* the shiver, as well as the way it made my belly flip.

You know better, I chastised myself. *These boys only want to play.*

I mean, Tray just tried to drown me yesterday. Sort of. Well, he looked a little concerned after, for all of a second. And he gave me a head start to get away. But he clearly meant to hurt me, just like Dash and Charlie. This was simply the mean clique's newest way to mess with me.

"I'm not going to Homecoming with you," I said, putting my foot down—literally—on his booted toes.

He didn't even flinch. No, the damn guy actually had the audacity to smile. "Then I guess we'll be failing together." He released me and fell back into his chair. "If you change your mind, let me know. I'll be having a nice little nap right here."

Tray closed his eyes.

And I growled.

"You can't make me attend a dinner and a dance just to pass this assignment."

His silence said otherwise.

I glanced around to see half the class observing our discord with keen interest; even Charlie appeared amused. "Cindersoot doesn't know how to dance, Nacht. Hell, she probably doesn't even know how to wear a dress."

That elicited several snickers and caused me to roll my eyes. "I'm wearing a skirt right now, Charlie Joe."

"Not the same as a dress, Ella Sewer," he returned. "But we all know it'd have to be a charity case from your sisters anyway."

"Stepsisters," I corrected. "And mind your own business." I kicked Tray's shoe, resulting in him opening one eye at me. "Dinner at six. No dance."

"Nope," he replied. "Dinner and the dance, and I want a list of questions tomorrow morning." He went back to his nap.

I muttered an obscenity in response just as Professor Montgomery flounced into the room, her gaze twinkling with excitement. "Good morning," she greeted us in a singsong voice, already taking over the class and forcing me back to my seat.

By the end of her hour-long lecture, I wanted to kill Trayton Nacht. The stubborn asshole was not going to leave me with any choice other than to accept his outlandish request. Otherwise, I'd forfeit the assignment grade, and I couldn't afford to do that.

I needed to maintain my grade point average to achieve my college goals of moving across the country and living far, far away from my evil stepsisters and stepmother. As all of my applications were currently under review, the last thing I needed was a failure on my record.

My teeth ground together, my stomach twisting in knots.

All right, I'd play his game.

I'd agree to dinner and the dance, and I'd make his life hell the entire time. Starting with my wardrobe choice. My lips tugged upward. Yeah, I had the perfect outfit in mind. If I was lucky, he'd finish our interview at the house as a result of not wanting to be seen in public with me.

"All right, Tray," I said to him, standing and pulling my bag onto my shoulder. "You win."

"Do I?" he asked, having paused midstep when I said his name. He glanced over his shoulder. "Six o'clock?"

"Six o'clock," I agreed.

"And the dance?"

I forced a smile. "Sure, Tray. We'll go to the dance."

His gaze twinkled. "You won't regret it."

I nearly snorted and instead just shook my head, leaving him behind me. Because yeah, he was right. I wouldn't regret this weekend at all. But he definitely would. I'd make sure of it.

"Don't forget your questions tomorrow," he called after me.

I flipped him off in response.
He'd get his interview questions.
And a hell of a lot more.

CHAPTER SIX

ISABELLA STOOD WAITING FOR ME at the front of her long, winding driveway in a pair of black ripped jeans and an oversized, ink-stained sweatshirt. Her blonde hair was tousled up into a messy bun, and her face was sans makeup.

My lips kicked up at the sides, amusement warming my chest.

If she thought this homeless look would turn me off, she had another think coming.

"Hello, darling," I said as I walked around the hood of my car. "Ready for your big night?"

Shock briefly widened her pupils, followed by a hint of intrigue as she took in the cut of my all-black suit. Her tongue slipped out to lick her lips, the little tell flooring me almost as much as her immediate recovery—when she narrowed her blue eyes into slits. "You consider Homecoming a big night?"

"I consider our first date a big night, yes." I opened the passenger-side door. "In you go, Isabella."

"Interview tip number one," she drawled, stepping forward in her beat-up boots. "I prefer Ella."

"Date tip number one"—I snagged her hip and pulled her to me so I could press my lips to her ear—"I'm calling you Isabella." I released her in the direction of the seat and smirked as she practically fell into the car. It wasn't my words so much as it was the baggy flare of her jeans. "Should have worn something a little more practical, beautiful."

She tucked her legs into the car and glared up at me. "Let's just get this over with."

"Sure." I shut her door, then picked up the bag she'd forgotten on the driveway to toss into my trunk. She'd already buckled herself in by the time I settled in beside her, not even bothering to thank me for retrieving her discarded belongings. "Your manners are exemplary," I told her as I started the car.

"Why, thank you," she replied, her tone sickly sweet. "I sharpened them just for you."

I snorted. "I actually believe that." She'd been prickly toward me all week, her interview sheet summing up her feelings toward me rather nicely.

What's your biggest failure?

Would you rather swim in a shark-infested pool or play in a snake pit?

Do you admire anyone more than yourself?

What's your least favorite kind of music?

Every question held a negative connotation, proving I had quite the fight on my hands here. Such a new experience from my usual. In the Midnight Fae Kingdom, all I had to do was glance at a female and she'd fall to her knees in happy oblivion.

But not with Isabella.

Oh, no. This girl was going to make me work for it. And I couldn't fucking wait.

We drove in silence to the restaurant I'd picked for our assignment. Isabella's attire was going to draw a lot of attention, something I suspected to be her goal. She probably expected her wardrobe to turn me off. Hence her resounding silence now. Actually, she seemed a little nervous, what with the way she kept picking at her nails.

I pulled up to the valet and fought a grin when Isabella stiffened beside me. "*La Scala?*" she asked, her voice a little breathy.

"Yep." I didn't give her a chance to say anything else as I exited the car and tossed my keys to the valet. She still hadn't moved when I opened her door, her seat belt firmly in place. "Ready?" I asked, holding out my hand for hers.

She glanced up at me, her cheeks a delicious shade of pink. "I... I'm not dressed for *La Scala*, Tray."

I cocked my head to the side. "You mean that's not your version of formal attire?"

She didn't smile or laugh or even glare. She just shook her head and focused on the windshield. "This was a mistake."

My brow furrowed. *Where's my feisty little female?* I wondered, crouching before her. "Isabella," I said softly, trying to grab her attention.

"Sir, I need—"

I shut the valet up with a wave of my hand. Literally. Dark magic pooled around him, knocking him into a daze of confusion that left him staring off into space. I'd deal with him in a moment.

"Ella," I tried again, this time using her preferred name. "It's just dinner."

"Not here." She closed her eyes. "Please not here."

Odd. This was supposed to be the fanciest place in town. It'd taken some magical strings for me to secure us a reservation, as half the senior class seemed to be dining here before the dance.

Was that why she didn't want to go inside?

My lips twisted to the side. No. That couldn't be it. She never let the other students intimidate her in class, so why would a restaurant be any different?

Regardless, she clearly wasn't comfortable, and while I didn't mind pushing her buttons, this seemed to go beyond mere teasing and into dangerous emotional territory. "Okay," I told her, standing up. "We'll go somewhere else."

I closed her door and waved my hand to release the spell on the valet. He blinked several times in confusion, the dark web slowly disentangling itself from his mind.

"Dinner was great," I said, handing him a tip in exchange for my keys. "Thanks, man."

He sputtered something unintelligible at my back that I ignored as I resettled into the driver's seat with a very quiet Isabella beside me.

She remained mute, leaving me to come up with the backup plan on my own. Darlington was full of expensive restaurants, the kind you paid a fortune for only to be hungry an hour later.

We needed something comfortable. Something low-key with decent food and an easy atmosphere.

Benji's, I thought, smiling. *Yes, that'll work.*

It was a local place one town over with the most amazing chicken wings. The perfect place for a casual date.

"Where are we going?" Isabella asked when we were nearing the outskirts of Darlington.

"To a local wing bar in Asherington," I said, my hand settling on the shifter between us as we neared a stoplight. I risked a glance at her and noted that her cheeks had returned to their usual pale color.

Her blue eyes drifted my way, blinking. "You're not going to ask me why?"

"Why what?" I hit the clutch to roll back into the right gear as the light color changed to green.

"Why I don't want to eat at *La Scala*."

I lifted a shoulder. "Your discomfort was all I needed to know, Isabella. If there's more you want to say, I'm listening. But I don't require an explanation."

She fell silent again, her attention on the autumn scenery outside. It wasn't until we were a few minutes from our destination that she picked up the conversation once more.

"Thank you," she whispered.

I didn't know if her gratitude was in reference to switching our location or for not asking questions. Perhaps both. Regardless, I nodded and replied, "You're welcome." Her comfort would always come first, a decision I'd made years ago.

I'd meant to bite her that fateful night, to sate the blood thirst my darker side required. But her essence had captivated me—part Midnight Fae, part human. A rare combination, marking her as a Halfling.

And she had no idea.

That would change very soon. I just needed to garner some trust first. It would help ease the acceptance of her birthright.

Well, that was the plan, anyway.

But something told me Isabella Cinder would never make it that easy.

I parked in the run-down lot outside Benji's and killed the engine. "Ready for the best chicken wings ever?" I asked.

She frowned at me. "You say that like you've eaten here many times before."

"Because I have," I admitted, jumping out of the car and wandering around to open her door.

She didn't freeze this time or stay seated, but her brows were drawn down as her feet met the concrete. "But you just moved here, right?"

I smiled. "Did I?"

"Uh, yeah. You just started at the academy this week."

After closing her door, I locked up the car. We could mess with our interview notes later.

43

"There's a lot you don't know about me, Isabella," I said, leading her toward the entrance. "Such as my obsession with Benji's wings."

"Where did you go to school before Darlington?" she asked, following me inside. "The local high school?"

I snorted. "No." I paused our conversation to give Belinda a little wave, and her lips curled into a welcoming grin from behind the bar.

She whistled, taking in my suit, and laughed. "You didn't need to get all dressed up on my account, hon."

"But you know how much I enjoy impressing you, Mrs. B."

She scoffed at that and gestured toward the booths along the side of the bar. "Take a seat wherever you want, Tray. You know the drill."

"Indeed I do," I replied, placing my palm against Isabella's back and steering her toward my favorite spot.

Her blue eyes drilled into mine after sliding into the seat across from me, the low lighting overhead glowing off her blonde hair. "Okay, so where did you live before if it wasn't in Darlington?"

"Cutting straight to the interview, are we?" I teased, sliding a menu across to her. "And you wouldn't believe me if I told you." I lifted my gaze to hers. "But if you behave tonight, perhaps I'll show you."

She scoffed. "Is that supposed to be a line to get me back to your place?" Her expression matched her retort. "Because that's not happening."

I covered my heart. "You wound me, Isabella."

"It's *Ella*, and I highly doubt that." She looked me over with an appraising glance. "We both know your pride is safe from the likes of me."

She couldn't be more wrong, but I chose not to argue her point and focused on another instead. "How about a deal," I proposed. "I'll call you Ella, as you clearly prefer, if you agree to at least give me a chance tonight. You've made a lot of assumptions for someone who has only met me a handful of times. I want a chance to prove some of those wrong."

"Yeah, I typically draw conclusions about a person after they try to drown me the first time," she replied, not missing a beat. "But sure. I'll let you try a second time, if it means getting my name right."

My lips twitched. "I didn't try to drown you, sweetheart."

"No?" Her eyebrows rose. "Was that your version of flirting, then?"

"It was my version of protecting you," I replied just as Belinda approached with two waters and a basket of peanuts. She read off the specials for Ella's benefit more than mine—I wanted wings and Mrs. B. knew it—and then left us to make our decisions.

But my date wasn't looking at the menu at all, her focus fully on me.

"You were trying to protect me by holding me underwater?" she asked, incredulous.

"If you don't look at the menu, I'm going to order wings for you," I warned her. "So I hope you like chicken."

"I don't care about food," she returned, crossing her arms. "I want to know how drowning me protects me."

Sighing, I braced my elbows on the table and leaned toward her. "It's a game, Ella. One I intend to control."

She blinked at me. "What? How? Why?"

"Because I want to keep you safe," I replied, gesturing for Belinda. "Give me tonight and I'll help you understand."

Mrs. B. arrived before Ella could utter a word. I ordered a variety of wings for us both, as well as cheese fries, celery sticks, and two cherry Cokes. Belinda shook her head, muttering something about where I put all the calories, and left us to our conversation.

Ella studied me intently, that brain of hers no doubt flying through a series of scenarios. "Why would you care about my safety?" she demanded.

"Because I like you," I admitted, leaning back into my

booth. "And I don't much care for Dash or Charlie."

"Yet you've been hanging out with them all week."

"Spying on me, dove?" I waggled my brows. "All you need to do is ask for my time and it's all yours."

She snorted. "Stop with the flirtatious diversions. What's your play here?"

"Who says they're diversions?" I countered, cocking my head. "And my play here is simple. I want you, Ella."

"Uh-huh." She narrowed those beautiful eyes at me. "Why?"

"Because you're special."

She gave me a look. "Seriously, that's the best you've got? At least Dash called me beautiful and commented on my intelligence. You're going with the bare minimum in an attempt to lure me to my humiliation." She leaned forward, her voice pitching low. "You'll have to do a lot better than that."

"Lure you to your humiliation," I repeated, mulling it over. "Now, see, I think you're playing this game all wrong, Ella."

"It's not a game."

"Everything in this world is a game, darling." She just hadn't realized it yet. "You're just reluctant to take on your role. But I can help you. And together, we'll win."

She arched a brow. "Win what?"

"The war between you and your evil-as-fuck stepsisters." I unbuttoned my jacket and spread my arms out across the back of my side of the booth, loving the way her eyes tracked every move. "By the time we're done, they won't know what hit them."

She contemplated for a moment, distrust a heavy emotion in her features. Considering our brief acquaintance, I couldn't blame her. And given everything she'd been through, she would need more than a few words from me to prove my point.

Which gave me an idea.

"How about this," I said, leaning forward once more and

lowering my voice. "Give me tonight. Let me show you what I have in mind. If you don't like it, we're done and I won't interfere in your circle anymore. But if you do like it"—which I knew she would—"we'll continue. And I promise that, by the end, your stepsisters will see justice for the hell they've put you through."

"You speak about my background like you know so much about me." Ella started tapping against the table, her expression skeptical. "Are you stalking me, Nacht?"

I grinned. "If I said I was, would you believe me?"

"I'd believe Ryan put you up to this crap," she replied, folding her arms across her chest. "That would explain your comment about my stepsisters putting me through hell."

"Or perhaps I'm observant and studied the school dynamics before transferring in." Which was exactly what I did.

"Okay, say I believe that." Her tone told me she absolutely did not believe it but was humoring me with a hypothetical situation. "What's in it for you? Why help me *seek justice*, as you put it."

"Because I like you, Ella."

"Right. Because I'm *special*." She used air quotes around the word. "I'm going to need more than that, Tray."

I scratched my stubbled jaw, considering what I could offer to change her mind. "You realize the reason your stepsisters are so hell-bent on tormenting you is because they're jealous, right?"

Her brow crinkled. "Jealous?" She released a humorless laugh. "Yeah, okay. Also, changing the subject won't improve my opinion of you."

"Don't worry. I'm working toward my explanation, darling." I paused to accept the drinks Belinda dropped off, then refocused on Ella. "You have the power to be the queen of Darlington Academy. It makes you a threat. That's why you're a target."

"Right, so clearly you've not been stalking me." She smiled, but it wasn't friendly. "They hate me because they

47

seem to think my father favored me."

"That's part of it, but not all of it," I argued. "You're gorgeous, Ella. Something they've gone out of their way to hide, but even Charlie and Dash still notice. Hell, everyone does. With my help, you could rule that school."

"And let me guess—you'd stand by my side in the process?"

I shrugged. "It'd be a benefit, yes." But my primary goal was to see those fuckers pay for what they'd done to her.

"Hard pass," she tossed back at me. "I have no desire to become *queen bee* of any academy."

Which only made her more perfect in my eyes.

Still… "You have no desire to make them pay for what they've done?"

"Again, you make it sound like you're familiar with my past." Suspicion glinted in her gaze. "Where did you move here from?"

"It doesn't take a genius to realize they've made your life a living hell," I countered, deflecting her inquiry. "What surprises me is how little you care about the possibility of getting revenge. Most would jump at the chance."

"Because I know it's futile."

"Do you?" I steepled my fingers on the table and captured her gaze. "Have you tried?"

"What would you suggest I do, Tray? They own the school." She lifted a brow as if to add, *And that's that.*

"But they don't own me."

"That remains to be seen," she replied coolly.

"Let me prove it to you tonight."

Her eyes rolled heavenward. "This again."

"My offer still stands," I murmured. "Give me tonight to show you what I mean. If you like it, we continue working together. If you don't, I'll leave you alone." At least in regard to seeking revenge. If she felt enough closure on the topic, then I wouldn't push it. Instead, I'd just escalate my timetable on her recruitment into the fae world.

Done.

She blew a strand of hair out of her face and shook her head. "All right, fine. If it means you'll leave me alone, I'll play along."

My lips curled. "Yeah?"

"Sure. Why not." She didn't sound the least bit excited, but I'd work on that. "So what's the plan? How are you going to change my mind?"

I smirked. If only she knew. "Well, for starters, I'm going to need you to change out of those clothes and into something more formal."

"That's going to be a problem."

"Why?"

"I don't own a dress," she replied, grimacing. "I'd have to borrow one from Ryan or Carmen, and…" She lifted another shoulder.

"It won't do you justice," I finished for her.

"I was going to say it won't fit."

That, too. "It's not a problem. I'll handle the dress. In fact, I'll handle it all. You just have to play along."

She arched a brow. "That sounds ominous, Nacht."

"On the contrary, *Cinder.* I'm about to make all your dreams come true. After we eat." Because I was starving. Then we'd begin.

CHAPTER SEVEN

WHAT ARE YOU REALLY UP TO, Trayton Nacht? I wondered for the thousandth time as I studied myself in the mirror. *And how the hell did you pull this off?*

Not only did he magically open a store for me to find a gown, but he also had a team come in to do my hair and makeup. I nearly protested the latter but decided the battle wasn't worth my time. If he wanted to waste his money on this extravagance, then so be it.

The only reason I indulged in this little game of his was to figure him out. He had to be doing this for his own benefit. Maybe Ryan or Charlie put him up to it. Some sort of twisted test to see how well he could humiliate me.

Well, the joke was on him.

Because he'd purchased this gorgeous dress and

probably spent a pretty penny on my hair and face. Oh, and the shoes. The silver stiletto heels gave me an extra two inches—which was nowhere near his over-six-foot height. All in all, I suspected he wasted a little over a thousand dollars on this princess charade.

At least I looked good.

The slight V in the neckline gave me a hint of cleavage while the bodice tapered into my slim waist, and the skirt flowed down to my ankles. I twirled in the mirror, watching as the fabric swooshed around my legs.

The blue ball gown was totally over the top for Homecoming.

I loved it.

And more importantly, Ryan and Carmen would hate it.

Two birds, one stone.

I just had to keep my wits about me to determine Tray's true motives, and it'd be a successful night. Well, apart from not knowing enough about him yet to write his biography. He was evasive at every turn, refusing to tell me where he attended school before the academy or how he had all these contacts throughout Darlington. It wasn't a large town, yet I'd never heard of him until this week. And it seemed Charlie and Dash hadn't either.

So who are you really? I thought as I picked up my blue clutch—another purchase I'd made just to round out Tray's bill—and started toward the exit to where Tray waited for me. He hadn't bothered to help with the dress selection or anything else, just introduced me to the team, handed over his card, and said he'd be outside if we needed anything.

As he'd set no limit to the expense, I had a little fun.

No, a lot of fun.

I wrapped my gloved fingers—another extravagant accessory—around the door handle and pulled it open.

Tray leaned against a limo parked next to the curb, his hands tucked into his suit pants and his focus on the starless night above. There was a hint of longing in his features, one that seemed to be distracting him from my arrival.

I cleared my throat to announce my presence.

He blinked and slowly drew his gaze to me, his irises reminding me of the black sky overhead as they heated in response to my attire. A slight shiver caressed my spine at the obvious approval in those dark, smoldering orbs. "You look gorgeous, Ella," he murmured.

I shrugged. "Yeah, it's amazing what a pound of makeup and a hairstylist can do. The dress isn't too bad either."

His lips curled as he shook his head, his messy auburn hair windblown from the incoming cold front. October in Massachusetts could go either way. Tonight seemed to be hinting at an icy winter to come.

Tray pushed off the limo, his eyes twinkling in the night as he stepped into my personal space to grab my hip. "It's not the accessories that make you beautiful, Ella. It's you." He pressed his lips to my temple before moving to the side to offer his arm. "Shall we?"

I wanted to protest his compliment, but I bit my tongue and nodded instead. We were almost to the part where he revealed his true intentions. I'd let him think I believed this silly little game until then.

"Thank you," I said as he helped me into the limo. My skirt took up half of the backseat, something that seemed to amuse him as he pushed some of the fabric aside to settle beside me. "What happened to your car?" I wondered out loud.

"Why? Do you prefer it over this extravagance?" he asked, picking up a platter of chocolate-covered strawberries and holding it out for me to pick one.

Indulging in one would ruin my lipstick. But I had a spare in my bag, thanks to the makeup lady. Another cost added to Tray's account, no doubt.

I set my clutch to the side, plucked a big berry from the center, and took a bite instead of replying to what I assumed was a rhetorical question on his part. It seemed Trayton Nacht preferred countering inquiries rather than actually answering them.

He watched as I finished the berry, his attention on my mouth. I licked the juice from my lips and took another treat. Because why not? They were good and I'd always enjoyed strawberries.

The limo began to move, causing butterflies to stir in my belly. We were almost two hours late for the dance, which meant everyone would be there when we arrived—something I suspected might be the point of all this.

I took a third strawberry and waved the rest away, not able to stomach any more. They were delicious, but my nerves were getting the best of me.

Tray set the plate aside and turned to me. "Are you ready for a little experiment, Ella?"

"Depends on the experiment," I replied, my insides twisting. Maybe the third berry was a bad idea. I shifted to place it on the platter and focused on him. "Why are you doing this?"

He chuckled. "I already told you why."

"I want your real reason, Tray." Because I didn't buy for one second that he just wanted to help me seek retribution. There had to be another motive. No one did things out of the goodness of their heart. And this guy barely knew me. "Who put you up to this?" I asked, taking a new path in my questioning. "Ryan? Carmen?"

He huffed a laugh and shook his head. "Give me tonight, Ella. I promise that, by the end, you'll understand."

Meaning he intended to reveal some of his cards at the dance.

Fine.

If he was hoping for a repeat performance of my breakdown from freshman year, he'd be disappointed. Fool me once, shame on you. Fool me twice, shame on me. And I wasn't particularly fond of the idea of being made a fool.

"I'm not like the others at your school," he added softly. "I'll prove it to you."

I shrugged, giving up. "Do your worst," I dared.

"How about my best instead?" he countered, arching a

brow.

I smoothed my gloved hands over my skirt. "Sure, Tray."

We rode the rest of the way in silence. The palatial location hosting this year's Homecoming seemed imposing and ominous as Tray assisted me out of the limo. Particularly with the way the sky hazed overhead, the clouds mingling with the moon high above. I half expected to see bats swirling around in the lamplights or an array of spiders climbing the stone walls. It would be appropriate for this time of year.

Alas, it was all decked out for the Homecoming dance Darlington Academy threw every fall on these decadent grounds. I wasn't sure who owned the estate, but it was at least a hundred years old with a hint of European influence in the architecture.

Tray pressed his palm to my lower back, guiding me up the stone stairs and toward the giant wooden doors. Two men popped out from behind the pillars at the top to pull on the handles for us, causing me to move closer to Tray's side. I hadn't even noticed them in their black uniforms, and I didn't particularly care for their abrupt appearance.

Pull it together, Ella, I told myself. *It's just a dance.*

Except the last time I attended one, I'd run off in tears after having my heart shattered in front of my entire class.

At least that hadn't happened *here.* That would have caused me to walk right back to the limo and demand Tray take me home.

But I could handle this.

Just breathe. Figure out what he's up to. And leave.

Those three orders repeated in my thoughts as we navigated the long hallway toward the thudding bass. There weren't a lot of decorations, mostly because the palace itself was already adorned in bronze and golds that boasted wealth and elegance in every corner. Even the marble floor appeared polished and rich. Floral arrangements mingled with low lighting, providing a romantic atmosphere that didn't quite match the modern music playing beyond.

Tray paused on the threshold of a platform at the end of the corridor, his gaze capturing mine. "Are you ready?"

The last time I stood in a position like this, it was only minutes before my inevitable humiliation. Hopefully, Tray would follow suit and show his true colors sooner rather than later. I was ready to get this over with and couldn't wait to put him right back in his place with my nonchalant reaction.

I refused to buy this whole helpful routine. Tray was definitely hiding something. Just like everyone else in this city.

"Ella?" He cupped my cheek, drawing me from my thoughts. "If you don't want to do this, we—"

"I'm fine," I cut in, forcing a tight smile. "Let's get this over with."

He chuckled and shook his head. "What every man wants to hear on a date."

"This isn't a date, Tray. It's a forced social experiment."

His laughter died as he stepped into my personal space—something he seemed to enjoy doing—and walked me backward into a wall. He settled his palms on either side of my head, effectively caging me. "You're right," he murmured, lowering his face until his lips were scant inches from mine. "This is just an introduction."

His mouth nearly brushed mine, only to skim my cheek as I turned my head at the last possible second. I felt his grin against my skin.

"Mmm, I like the way you play," he whispered, his nose trailing along my jaw to my neck. The light touch drew goose bumps to the surface, eliciting a quiver from deep within. It was a direct contrast to the heat licking a path up my spine and settling in my chest.

"I'm not playing," I replied, my voice hoarse to my ears.

He chuckled against my throat, his breath awakening a flutter of butterflies in my lower abdomen.

What is it with this guy? I wondered, pressing back into the wall and striving for distance. Charlie and Dash had done things like this to me before, but not quite. With them, I just wanted to shove them away. With Tray… some twisted part of me wanted to grab him. To touch him in return. To arch into him rather than cower against the surface behind me.

His teeth skimmed my pulse, causing my heart to skip a beat.

My fingers curled into my palm. "Tray…" I didn't know what I wanted to say, couldn't think beyond the way his body felt pressing into mine.

Hot.

Burning.

Need.

I swallowed, my eyes drifting closed. This wasn't supposed to happen. No, this *couldn't* happen. I needed to wake the heck up, to push him away just like I did with Dash and Charlie. Trayton Nacht was not into me. This—

"Ella," he whispered, his tongue tracing the column of my neck up to my ear and dismantling my focus once more.

I'm so screwed.

"This might not be a real date, but there's something between us," he continued, nipping my earlobe and stealing my ability to speak. Not that I would know how to reply to him. "We're going to walk down those stairs so everyone can see the princess beneath the façade. And by the time we're done with these miscreants, they'll all bow at your feet."

He palmed my cheek to guide my gaze up to his, that alluring mouth of his far too close to my own. "Are you ready?" he asked.

I couldn't seem to breathe properly, so I just nodded. We needed to get this over with so I could go home. Quickly.

A "rip off the Band-Aid" sort of approach. Like, right now. And run. Run far—

He lightly touched his lips to the edge of my mouth, short-circuiting my thoughts again. And then released me.

A retort caught in my throat, the words gibberish by the time I forced them into my mouth. So I swallowed them and shook my head, trying to knock some sense back into myself.

This guy was potent.

A walking hazard who scrambled my brain cells.

A threat I needed to get far away from. Which was precisely the opposite thing that I did as he extended his elbow. My body acted of its own volition, my arm treacherously looping through his as he led me toward the platform.

What is happening to me? I wondered, feeling lighter than air on my heels. *He kissed me.*

What a ludicrous thought. Why should that matter? Dash had kissed me, too. Several times. But I never felt like *this* afterward.

And, wait, Tray really didn't kiss me. Not passionately.

So why the heck was I floating on cloud nine over here? Because a cute guy touched me? I frowned. That cute guy also tried to drown me this week. And I wasn't buying his protection act for a minute.

My stupid body just hadn't received the mental memo yet.

Hence my legs moving us down the stairs into the ballroom below.

Where half my class seemed to be standing, all of their eyes round and on us. Great. Tray would be making his scene any second now.

"You're stunning," he whispered against my ear. "And now everyone knows it."

I didn't bother replying to that. Impressing me would take a whole hell of a lot more than a few measly compliments. And this dress. And the limo. And everything else he'd done tonight.

Shaking myself once more, I refocused on our surroundings. Ryan stood beside a scowling Dash, her expression souring as she took in my blue gown. Carmen appeared behind her with an equally irritated look. Very different from my last dance, where they'd positively beamed at my entrance.

So what was different about tonight?

Tray steered me away from them and toward the center of the room, his lips falling to my ear again. "Dance with me."

"Why?" I asked, shivering from his nearness and the multitude of eyes on me. I thought I could do this, face all my classmates and essentially tell them to go screw themselves. But Tray had unnerved me, his touch confusing my sensibilities.

"Because everyone is staring at us and I want to give them something to really look at," he replied, swinging me into his arms in an expert move that my feet automatically followed.

Ballroom dancing was an elective course at the academy. But that wasn't how I knew how to respond. My mother had taught me the formal movements at a very young age. She'd also enrolled me in ballet—my favorite activity until my step-monster took it from me. *Chores are more important than gallivanting around in slippers*, she'd said.

My heart ached at the thought. But my pulse quickly escalated as Tray nudged my hips in a way I hadn't felt in years.

I followed as he led, my legs and torso moving as if under a spell of my past life. Memories of my mother whirled through my mind, just as they had outside of *La Scala*. Only, it wasn't pain I felt this time, but freedom.

I'm dancing, I marveled, temporarily suspended in a frame of mind I hadn't felt in so, so long. How Tray maneuvered me into this position, I couldn't say. But now that I was here, I didn't want to leave.

I felt alive.

Like a bird soaring through the sky.

Flying.

Free.

He picked up our pace, matching the rhythm of the song beautifully and turning me at all the right moments. His hands expertly led mine, his footing a master of perfection, and I lost myself to the music. Gave in to Tray and his expert skill. Allowing myself to forget the cruel world around us, to pretend we thrived in another world entirely.

His palms were a brand against my waist, then my hips, and on my lower back. I felt possessed by him, owned utterly by the fluttering of sound guiding our steps. He dipped me to the ground and back up, my chest heaving against his own, as the sound of applause pierced my ears.

Smoldering dark brown irises held mine.

No smile.

No amusement.

Just an intensity that nearly burned me alive.

I swallowed, uncertain of how this all happened. It was as if he'd woven a spell over me, controlling my actions and dissolving my hesitation.

His fingers trailed up my spine to caress the back of my neck while his opposite hand settled on my hip. "Now they see the real you, Ella," he whispered. "A glistening jewel in a sea of darkness."

I blinked at him. "You say the strangest things to me."

"And I've only gotten started, sweetheart." His mouth settled over mine so quickly that I didn't understand what he was doing until his tongue parted my lips.

The world froze around me.

Because that brush of his mouth in the hallway before was nothing compared to *this*. He kissed me as if his life depended on mine to survive. I couldn't breathe beneath the intensity, the *ownership* of his touch.

Some part of me knew to fight.

While the other part sighed at the rightness of his caress. *I'm going insane.*

I shouldn't be embracing him, yet I was. Vigorously, too. I even had my fingers in his hair. My damn body taking charge without my mind's permission. But I was too wrapped up in his touch to stop it, everything and everyone lost to the white noise of my thoughts.

His tongue moved against mine with the same skill he'd used to guide me around the dance floor, hypnotizing me into submitting.

A loud ding sent a jolt down my spine, drawing me back to reality like a slap across my face. It came from a clock somewhere in the ballroom, announcing the time. *Midnight.*

My eyes slid open to find a circle around us.

Just like that night freshman year.

Dread pooled in my belly.

A foreboding sensation crawling across my skin.

Tray smiled at someone over my shoulder, and my heart stopped. *Three, two...*

"Well, this looks cozy," Ryan said from behind me. "I barely even recognized you, Cindersoot. What with the makeover and all."

Carmen cackled, the sound sending a chill down my spine. "Still can't hide the trash beneath."

One of them fondled the skirt of my dress, and I knew what they planned to do next. Even before I heard the telltale sound of a rip.

Shit.

CHAPTER EIGHT

ELLA

"LADIES," Tray greeted, his palms falling to my hips to hold me in place. "Have you come to collect?"

"Hmm, depends on what you're offering," Ryan replied as a nail slid sharply up my back to the top of my zipper.

Tray spun me in his arms before I could react, my dress remaining upright as a result. "I owe your stepsister a dance," he murmured against my ear. "Go grab us some drinks." He pushed me to the side, stepping forward at the same time to draw Ryan into his arms.

I blinked at his back, shocked despite knowing something like this would happen. It just wasn't how I expected it to go down. A public humiliation, sure, but swapping dance partners?

"Now, Isabella," he added, glancing at me over his

shoulder.

Carmen and Ryan snickered while I narrowed my gaze at him.

He wanted me to go fetch them some drinks like a dog? Okay. Sure. I could do that. "I'll be right back," I said sweetly, seething inside.

How had I fallen beneath his spell so easily? He'd *kissed* me in front of all these people. Would he do the same with Ryan now? Was that his endgame—to show exactly how dispensable I was to him? Or maybe he planned to tell everyone I didn't live up to his standards, to try to embarrass me on an intimate level.

Regardless, I wouldn't be giving him the satisfaction.

He could dance all night with Ryan, for all I cared. But first, I'd grab their *drinks*.

My lips twitched at the plan forming in my head, only to walk nearly headfirst into Dash and Charlie, who stood on the sidelines waiting for me. I knew better than to shove past them, so I stopped and arched a brow. "Yes?"

"I see the attire hasn't improved your manners," Charlie drawled, his gaze raking over my dress and pausing far too long on my neckline.

Dash circled me, his expression boasting a rare serious quality. He usually smirked or glared or said something derisive, but he appeared quiet and contemplative tonight. That almost made me more nervous.

"Did you two want something?" I demanded, my hands on my hips.

"Yes." Dash grabbed my wrist. "A dance."

I nearly snorted. He couldn't be serious. "Sure," I lied. "After I get His Majesty the drinks he requested, we can dance."

Not.

I would be leaving just as soon as I finished playing fetch for the aspiring prince of Darlington Academy. I mean, wasn't that his rationale for helping me? He'd said he wanted to stand by my side when I took over as the new queen. But why bother when he could go after the current monarch?

Dash's grip tightened. "*Ella.*"

I blinked at him. "Sorry, what?" He'd clearly been speaking when I lost my train of thought.

He tugged me closer as Charlie stepped into my back, effectively trapping me between them. "I want to dance."

Their crowding held a lethal edge that had my heart skipping a beat. *Stay calm,* I coached myself. *Try to smile.* "We will just as soon as I finish grabbing His Majesty's drinks."

His resulting frown told me he didn't approve of my response. "It wasn't a request."

"I think we need to remind her who's in charge here, Charming."

"I think we do, too, Anderson," he agreed, releasing my wrist to palm my lower back. "Don't you remember our first dance, Cindersoot? How much fun we had together?"

My eyes narrowed. "Yeah. Fun. That's what I remember having."

"Do you need me to kiss you again? To remind you what it felt like to be in my capable hands?" He demonstrated by lowering said hand to my ass and squeezing. Hard.

Charlie leaned in to bite my ear, causing me to yelp in surprise. "Maybe you'd rather experience my mouth for a change."

I shivered—and not in a good way. "No, thank you," I said, trying to twist out from between them.

Hands clamped around my middle, holding me in place as Dash lowered his face to hover over mine. "I'm tired of this cold-bitch routine, darling." He captured my chin between his fingers, pinching to the point of pain. "If you can kiss Tray, you can kiss me."

"I kiss who I want to kiss," I retorted, spitting in his face when his lips came a little too close to mine. I'd rather deal with his physical wrath than allow that foul mouth anywhere near mine.

He growled low in his throat, his grip tightening to an

agonizing degree while his opposite hand fisted in my dress, yanking me forward. "Lick it off, bitch."

"Lick it off yourself, jackass." I lifted my knee, hoping to connect with his groin, only to have my limb tangled in the tulle of my skirt. *Damn ball gown!*

He rubbed his face against mine while Charlie gripped my hips, holding me still. I gagged in response to both the erection pressing into my backside and the slimy substance spreading across my cheek.

Ugh, and as usual, no one came to my defense.

People just watched because this entire academy housed a flock of rich sheep.

And the teachers were fuck knew where.

I only had myself to rely on, as always.

Being manhandled by *two* guys. Oh, but they were the princes of the school, captains of their respective sports teams, so obviously no one could do a damn thing about them. No. Not Charlie Anderson or Dash Charming.

Flames practically licked my veins, heating my skin to a boiling point as I fought in earnest to release their holds.

Which only made them laugh.

They loved when I struggled.

"Release me," I demanded.

"Oh, come on, Cindersoot. You wore this dress to impress us, and it worked. Deal with it." Dash was the picture of calm arrogance, his lips curling into a devious grin. "Tell us what you're wearing beneath. Something lacy and blue, just like this gown?"

"Mmm, or maybe nothing at all," Charlie suggested, his lips far too close to my ear as he ground his arousal into my ass.

"Enough," I snapped, trying and failing to twist out from between them. They had me well and truly trapped. My heart leapt into my throat. *At least we're not alone*, I tried to tell myself. *Yeah, like anyone else is going to care or help.*

I had to play this smart.

Give them what they wanted and lull them into a sense

of comfort until I could escape.

That was the—

"Get your hands off my date," a cool voice demanded from a few steps away.

Oh, good. *He* wanted to pretend to be a knight. As if I would ever fall for that. "Fuck off, Tray," I told him, furious at everyone and everything. "Go back to your new queen."

With Dash continuing to hold my chin, I couldn't see Tray's facial reaction, but I heard the laugh that fell from his lips. "I see you've riled her up," he said conversationally.

"It's so easy to do," Charlie replied, pressing his nose into my hair. "Do we have you to thank for her improved conditions?"

"I may have hired a team of makeup artists and a hairstylist," he admitted, holding out his hand. "Come here, Ella."

I wouldn't acknowledge that even if I could.

"We're not done playing with her yet." Dash tilted his head, his eyes holding mine. "She seems to think she has the right to refuse me."

"When she's my date to a dance, I'd agree that she most certainly does have that right," Tray countered, an edge entering his tone. "Release my date, Charming. You had your fun with her. It's my turn now."

"On the contrary, I think you're done and it's time to leave her with the professionals." Dash slammed his mouth into mine, his tongue shoving between my lips before I had a chance to even process his movements.

My teeth clamped down in protest, my body freezing.

A completely opposite reaction to Tray's kiss, something I'd evaluate later.

But Dash? I wanted him off me. Right. Fucking. Now.

I planted my palms against his chest and shoved as hard as I could, but his muscular form didn't budge an inch.

Until someone ripped him backward. The abrupt movement cracked my frozen shell and spun me into action as I whirled on Charlie and sent my fist into his nose.

Tray caught me around the waist, hoisting me into the air and spinning me behind him. "Stay," he snapped, turning to face the two assholes he'd just wrangled me out from.

If he thought I intended to listen to his command, he had another think coming.

I took off through the ballroom, ignoring Ryan's and Carmen's shouts at my back, and sprinted up the stairs toward the exit.

Fuck him.

Fuck Dash.

Fuck Charlie.

Fuck Ryan.

Fuck Carmen.

Fuck Darlington Academy.

Fuck this entire fucking city!

June could not come fast enough.

I pushed through the front doors, kicked off the stiletto heels because they were slowing me down, and ran barefoot down the cobblestone drive. It hurt, but I'd numbed myself to the pain years ago.

Surviving the death of my parents and the perpetual treatment of the *family* that was supposed to care for me had ensured that I had the mettle of steel. I could handle a little blood and cuts.

"Isabella!" Tray shouted behind me, sending a shiver down my spine. But unlike the shiver Charlie and Dash had elicited, this one left me feeling warm inside.

Which I hated even more.

Why did my body react to Tray in this manner? Sure, he was hot. But so were the other douchebags, and they didn't leave me feeling hot all over.

Pushing the thoughts from my mind, I urged my legs to move faster, but the damn skirts continued to tangle with my limbs, slowing me down. If I moved too quickly, I'd trip, and then—

Strong arms circled my core, hoisting me into the air and off my feet.

I shrieked, the trees and limos my only witnesses.

Surely one of the drivers would come forward. Right?

Oh, no. I forgot. I lived in Darlington, where employees were paid to be discreet and look the other way.

I screamed in frustration, my anger at fate hitting a high point. "Why?!" I shouted at no one in particular. And a slew of curses followed.

Tray said nothing.

Or maybe I just couldn't hear him over my own screams.

I wasn't crying for help but ranting at the heavens for their cruelty.

Eight. Fucking. Months.

I had to survive eight more fucking months. And I wasn't sure I could without killing someone.

"I can help with that." The soft words came from Tray, and I glared at him over my shoulder.

"Help with what?" I demanded.

"Killing them all. If that's what you want."

I scoffed. "Yeah, right. Why are you even here?" I tried to squirm out of his hold with little success.

"You're not running away from me again, Isabella."

I rolled my eyes and huffed a humorless laugh. "Right." I attempted again to shove away from him, and he spun me in his arms. Smoldering black orbs flickered with embers as he glowered down at me, the abnormal effect stealing the breath from my lungs.

Because that definitely wasn't normal.

Eyes didn't… *flame.*

But a fire danced in his irises now, lighting up his features and lending an unearthly appeal to his handsome face.

And is that smoke billowing around him?

I blinked, trying to dismiss the black tendrils rolling off his suit. Only, they intensified the longer I stared.

"I wanted to do this another way, to ease you into your birthright, but tonight proved that's not going to happen. Any and all foundations of trust have been long bullied out of you. So we'll go about this the hard way." He relaxed his hold, but not enough for me to escape. Not that I could. No, after that proclamation, my feet refused to budge.

I ignored the bully crap and focused on the part that cemented me to the ground before him. "What are you talking about? What birthright?"

"The one bestowed upon you by your mother's bloodline," he replied, releasing me as a limo came to a stop beside us. "Get in and I'll explain."

My eyebrows inched upward. "Yeah, hard pass. You'll explain here. Right now."

Annoyance flickered in his features. "I'm really starting to regret my approach to this entire situation. If you knew who I was from the beginning, you wouldn't dare question an order."

"Yeah? Well, I'm pretty sure I'd be questioning you regardless." I folded my arms. "Start talking."

He opened the door and faced me, his eyes swirling a hypnotic shade of black and orange. "Step forward, Isabella," he murmured, the words seeming to wrap around me and tug at my spirit to comply.

How... strange...

I yelped as my feet moved, my mind rebelling even as my body followed his command.

"Good girl," he said softly. "Now settle yourself in the car and don't scream. I already have a headache."

I opened my mouth to protest, but the world fell into a haze around me.

Is this a dream? I wondered, pinching my side. *Did Charlie or Dash knock me out?*

Because this couldn't be happening.

There was no way I'd just get into the limo without putting up a fight. Yet I *felt* the leather seat beneath me, sensed Tray's warmth as he slid in beside me, and heard the door slam.

How is he doing this? I blinked in an attempt to clear the fog from my mind. My head lolled, sleep seeming to override my senses.

"What are you doing to me?" I whispered, fighting the cloud suffocating my thoughts. *Did he drug me?* No. I didn't drink anything.

"Relax, Isabella."

Ella, I thought at him.

"You'll understand soon." His fingers combed through my hair, the pins releasing from the top of my head as he helped dismantle my updo. "I'm not going to hurt you."

Some of the haze lifted, bringing the limo back into focus. A flurry of trees lined the roads outside, the palatial grounds long gone.

Wait…

I peered through the glass, frowning at the unfamiliar ivy twining along the ground.

We couldn't be that far from the Homecoming dance. But I recognized nothing outside.

"Where are we?" I demanded, pleased to hear my voice sounding somewhat normal.

"On our way to my home," he replied. "My *real* home."

"You're taking me back to your place?" I nearly laughed. "Wow. No. I refuse."

"It's too late for that, Isabella." He removed the final pin from my hair, allowing it to clink into a cup holder.

"*Ella,*" I snapped at him. "Only my parents are permitted to call me Isabella, and they're dead."

He flinched at my words, clearly not expecting the venom in my tone.

The nerve of this guy.

"Take me home, *Trayton*."

"I am," he replied. "Well, sort of."

"You just said we're going to your house."

"No, I said we're going to my home." He relaxed into his seat, appearing far too regal in his suit. "You wanted to know who I am, and I'm about to show you."

I opened my mouth to argue, when an odd flicker of light caught my attention, distracting me. *A moon,* I realized, staring out into the night. *No. Not a moon.* Two *moons.*

"What the…?" I gaped outside at the myriad of stars twinkling in the sky between the gold globes. "That's not possible."

And neither was all this ivy.

It seemed to be moving, reminding me of slithering green snakes traveling up and around the branches.

Red pinpoints stared back at me, watching the limousine wind down the unending road.

No other cars.

No houses.

Just endless forest with the startling night sky overhead.

My earlier thoughts about this being a dream settled over me once more.

"It's real, Ella." Tray reached for my hand, giving it a squeeze before I ripped it from his grip.

"Start talking," I demanded, chills sweeping up and down my body. "Right now, Tray. I mean it. I need you to tell me what the hell is going on."

CHAPTER NINE

TRAY

WELL, TONIGHT'S GONE TO SHIT, I thought, running my fingers through my hair and blowing out a breath.

I'd underestimated the pettiness of the humans at Darlington Academy. Particularly, Ryan.

The envy in that chick had nearly spoiled all my plans. When I heard her begin to rip Ella's dress, I'd reacted in the only way I could—by retraining Ryan's focus on me and away from her stepsister. Only, Charlie and Dash had jumped at the chance to harass beautiful Ella, their interaction bordering on sexual assault.

There was no doubt in my mind that tonight they would have taken it further than ever before. All because I'd dressed her up and provided her with a space to shine, thinking it would serve as gleeful retribution against her classmates.

Except it all backfired.

Those jackasses had been raised without principles, and my actions painted an even larger target on her back, essentially provoking the bastards into coming out to play.

I meant what I said to her in the car park. If she wanted to kill them, I'd gladly help.

And that included her bitchy stepsisters.

Shit. I should have known Ryan wouldn't go along with our agreed-upon charade, choosing to take the moment into her own hands to try to ruin her stepsister thoroughly. Instead, it ended in me pushing Ella away and giving everyone the impression I'd chosen Ryan over her.

I wanted to slam my fist through the glass, to rage at the stupidity of these human nuances, but I had a very shaken female beside me who had just realized we weren't in her realm anymore.

And that was a completely different bucket of problems to work through. Not only had I compelled her tonight to follow my orders, but I'd also taken her into the Midnight Fae world without her permission.

She had every right to hate me, and I had no doubt that she would by the time the night was through.

"*Tray,*" she said, the emotion in her voice piercing my heart. Isabella Cinder was incredibly strong, her courage one I admired more than she knew. But tonight had done a number on her, and I wasn't going to make it any better.

No, I was about to make it a hell of a lot worse.

With a resigned sigh, I met her gaze. "We met once, several years ago in an alley. You were soaking wet and freezing to death and ran right into me while wearing a dress and matching blue slippers." The color of which wasn't much different from the one she wore now, suggesting it might be her favorite shade.

I bent to pick up her silver stilettos that she'd shucked off near the doors tonight and handed them to her. "You have a penchant for losing your shoes, Isabella Cinder."

Her face paled. "It was you that night?"

I nodded.

"And you're just now telling me?" She snatched the heels from my hands and dropped them unceremoniously onto the floor. "No, forget that. I want to know where the hell we are and why the ivy outside keeps moving."

"It's not ivy. They're magicked vines that protect our grounds from intruders." I looked over her shoulder at the trees. "I believe humans would liken them to snakes, but our version is far more deadly. They won't just bite and squeeze; they'll enchant and drain energy. Terrifying, really, if you're an unwanted guest."

Her eyes closed, opened, closed, and opened once more. "What?"

"You asked; I answered." I shrugged. "You're about to see a lot of things that are hard to believe, Ella." I snapped my fingers, drawing a flame to the surface and flicking it into the air. A parlor trick for a Dark Fae my age, but it elicited the requisite gasp from my companion.

"H-how did you do that?"

"Magic, sweetheart." I waved my hand while muttering a spell under my breath and smiled as a black rose appeared in my palm. Seemed appropriate considering our *date*.

I held it out for her and she scooted away, her eyes wide. "What. The. Fuck?"

"I'm a fae, Ella. Well, formally known as a Midnight Fae due to my darker heritage. A royal by blood. Just like you, only we come from different familial lines." Which was a good thing or this attraction I felt for her would be wrong on several levels.

More blinking, her mouth opening and closing without sound.

However, disbelief practically poured from her exterior. Which was precisely why I brought her here. The only way she'd believe me would be to *see*.

I took advantage of her silence and continued my explanation. "Your mother was a fae, but she fell in love with a human—your father. It's not common among our kind, particularly among the royal sect, but it's not unheard of. I mean, Midnight Fae interact with mortality to sate our blood thirst. It's what sets us apart from other fae. Well, that and our favor with the dark arts, necromancy, and other—"

"Hold on," she said, lifting her hand. "Blood thirst?"

I smirked. "Of all the things I said, that's what you chose to hear?" Typical human. "Yeah, we drink human blood. And before you freak out, it's not often. Just enough to keep our darker elements alive. That's how I know about Darlington and the surrounding suburbs. It's my preferred feeding ground." I met her gaze. "And you were my target the night we met." Only, I'd been so startled by her Halfling nature that I'd been unable to perform, let alone bite her.

Her eyes were as wide as saucers. "*You're a vampire?*"

I snorted. "Hardly. You've seen me eat, Ella. And you've seen me in sunlight. Also? Vampires don't exist. They're a myth contrived by humans, likely because of a few idiot Midnight Fae who didn't compel their prey correctly."

"Compel?" she repeated, understanding brightening her features. "You *compelled* me tonight."

"Yeah, I did," I admitted, running my fingers through my hair. "Not that it's a great excuse, but you wouldn't have gotten in the car without it." I'd seen the fight written all over her body, and I wasn't in the mood to persuade via my usual charms. They were all burned out, thanks to Ryan and her damn shenanigans.

"And the dancing," she added.

My eyebrow lifted. "What about the dancing?"

"You compelled me then, too."

It took me a moment to realize what she really meant— the seduction and subsequent kiss. Amusement tilted my lips. "Oh, no, sweetheart. That was real. No compulsion involved."

"You made me kiss you."

"I assure you, I did no such thing." I leaned forward,

crowding her against the door. "I've never compelled a woman to touch me, Ella. There's never been a need, nor would I desire it. Besides, part of the fun is the foreplay. Why would I belittle such a thing by adding compulsion to the mix?" I wasn't Dash or Charlie. When I craved a female, I worked for it. And tonight was no different.

"You expect me to believe you?"

"No," I replied without missing a beat. "In fact, I fully anticipated you *not* believing me, which is why I brought you here."

"I'm talking about the compulsion, Trayton."

I tongued my teeth, considering how I wanted to reply to that. "If it makes you feel better to believe I'm lying, then I'll allow it." Because my conscience in this regard was clear. "However, deep down, you know the truth already, Ella. Because you have *real* compulsion to compare it to."

Her gaze narrowed and she glanced out the window, only to shudder and face forward. Because yeah, the vines were growing agitated. They sensed her discontent and likely ill thoughts toward me. As a royal of these grounds, the enchantment would do what was required to protect me against any and all threats.

Interesting that it considered Ella a threat when she clearly didn't have access to her powers yet. Which was an oddity in and of itself. Midnight Fae were born with their gifts. Halflings came into them over time, but she should have access to her inner strengths by her eighteenth birthday—an event that had come and gone.

"Your mother was powerful," I said, thinking out loud. "Renowned, actually." It was entirely possible she'd enchanted her daughter in some capacity, but I hadn't picked up on any dark-magic notes from Ella. In fact, I hadn't detected a single note of power inside her. Just a very strong resolve and a courage that would put most fae to shame.

"My mother," she whispered, her attention shifting to her hands. "Did you know my mother?"

"No, but my parents did. They all grew up together in the royal circuit and attended Midnight Fae Academy around the same time."

"Midnight Fae Academy?" she repeated.

I nodded. "It's where our kind go to perfect our access to the dark arts. Our scores and knowledge then determine where we end up in the society sects. It's sort of like your version of college, only for Midnight Fae."

"So why are you in Darlington?" she asked.

"Because I've been assigned to recruit you, Ella."

And you're my intended mate, I added mentally. *Welcome to the family.*

We'd cover that aspect later.

After she understood everything else.

"You're part Midnight Fae," I continued. "The Council expects you to attend the Academy next year." And they wouldn't be taking no for an answer. Another item to explain later. After I had a chance to thaw her a little to the Midnight Fae life.

The limo slowed as we approached the estate's main gates. Stone gargoyles guarded the walls, their eyes alert and scanning for danger just like the vines.

Ella gaped up at them, goose bumps filing down her arms and disappearing into the gloves she still wore. "They're moving," she whispered.

"Yes. They're gargoyles." And unlike the ones humans enjoyed as ornaments or decorations, these were very much real.

"Do they fly?"

"Only when going on the attack." Which never happened. A fae would have to be suicidal to approach these grounds with negative intent. My father was the Midnight Fae King. He took his security very seriously.

We continued down another winding path after being permitted through the gates, Ella's undivided attention on the changing surroundings.

Black water lakes reflecting the light.

Acres of stones and trees intertwined.

Walking paths.

"Is that a phoenix?" she breathed, eyeing a firebird in the distance.

"Similar," I replied. "Not as big as the ones from your legends. The firebirds only grow as large as your standard eagle."

"Right." She visibly shuddered. "This..."

"Is real," I finished for her.

"Uh-huh," she replied, eyeing a horde of water sparks dancing over the lake. "Fairies?"

I grunted. "More like gnats, only larger and they sting. I definitely don't recommend touching one." Unfortunately, they were an infestation that couldn't be eradicated even with magic.

"And you're a fae," she said slowly.

"As are you," I returned.

She glanced at my head, frowning. "Your ears are round."

I gave her a look. "As are yours, Ella."

"I thought fae had pointed ears."

"Some do," I agreed. "Midnight Fae do not."

"So there are other types of fae?"

I nodded. "Many, yes. This is just one realm of several."

"Oh." She went back to staring out the window, her shoulders stiff. "Do they all drink blood?"

"Only Midnight Fae because of our access to the dark arts."

"Why?" she pressed. "Why only Midnight Fae?"

"Because it fuels our access to the dark arts," I explained patiently. This was a lot for her to take in, so there would be some necessary repetition in responses. "Some see it as a moral punishment to satiate the harsher side of our existence. Others embrace it as a sustenance to fuel our energy reserves."

"And how do you view it?" she glanced at me. "And how often do you... you know?"

"It's a natural part of our existence that I accepted long ago, and I feed once a month or so. It's not often and it doesn't require much. And before you ask, no, we don't kill humans. We just borrow some of their life energy every now and then. Most of them live to enjoy it." Blood exchange tended to result in heightened sexual sensations. Something I would eventually need to explain. Or maybe I'd show her, if she let me.

"I see." She bit her lip, her brow drawing down. "I don't drink blood."

"Because you're a Halfling without access to your powers." But that did bring up a potential explanation for *why* she hadn't shown signs of her gifts yet. Perhaps it was a result of her not drinking blood. I'd have to ask my father or maybe my brother, Kols, later for an opinion.

Ella stiffened as the official Nacht Estate appeared, the lights shining starkly against the night and illuminating the vast columns and granite exterior.

Her jaw dropped a little. "It's like a gothic palace."

I chuckled. "Only on the outside." The inside was all clean, modern lines, thanks to my mother's penchant for elegance. "You're about to see a lot of silver and gold." Those were the family colors, with a hint of black woven into the crest. "And probably a lot of magic, too," I added, grimacing.

"Because we're in a fae world," she replied.

"Midnight Fae Realm, yes."

She nodded, shook her head, and nodded again. "Uh-huh."

"You're allowed to freak out, Ella."

"Yep." Another one of those odd nod-shakes again. "Yep."

"Ella."

"I'm fine," she said quickly. "Really. I mean, I'm totally *not* fine. But I'm also fine."

"Because that's a coherent statement," I drawled.

She narrowed her gaze at me. "You just abducted me

78

and whisked me to a fae realm, and you want to poke fun at my reaction? Now? Really?"

I lifted my hands while adoring the appearance of her feisty attitude. "That's fair. I'm just saying you're allowed to freak out. I'll understand."

"And what good would it do?" she countered, folding her arms. "Other than putting me at your mercy even more than I already am."

"Also fair," I agreed. "If it's any consolation, I don't plan to keep you here. We're just visiting for the night as a way to prove to you that I'm not full of shit. Then, tomorrow, we'll head back to Darlington."

"What?" She openly gaped at me. "So, wait, you only brought me here to... prove this all to me?"

"Essentially, yeah. I could tell that nothing I said tonight would convince you I'm not trying to hurt you, so I figured I'd reveal it all at once. And then, hopefully, we can move forward."

"And do what?" she demanded. "Go back to high school?"

"Yeah," I said pinning her with a look. "Except this time you'll be armed with the knowledge that I actually do want to help you put those assholes in their place."

Because they needed to pay for their sins and I refused to do it on Ella's behalf. She would only obtain true closure if she did it for herself.

"So maybe you'll be a little more agreeable this time around," I added, more irritated at myself than at her.

"More agreeable," she repeated. "Why do you even care? I mean, I get the assignment part. But *fae are real.* You're like a vampire. Why the hell would you voluntarily enroll in a human high school just to play with a bunch of rich, spoiled brats?"

Because those rich, spoiled brats fucked with my intended mate and I want to make them suffer for it, I thought.

Unfortunately, I couldn't say that. Not without freaking her out even more.

So I went with the next best reason, which also happened to be true.

"Because something is blocking your powers from surfacing and I suspect it's related to the emotional armor you created to survive all these years of abuse." I met her gaze. "Had I intervened when we first met, perhaps things would have turned out differently. But I waited until you were eighteen, as the Council recommended, and you've endured hell in my absence. So as your assigned guardian, I've failed you. And I won't rest until I've made this right."

CHAPTER TEN

ELLA

AS FAR AS REASONS WENT, that was a good one. So good, in fact, that I didn't know how to reply to him.

Which was why I kept my mouth shut until we were parked outside the gothic palace Tray called home.

A fae. A real fucking fae.

And he was right.

I would never have believed him without seeing all of this. Even now, some part of me desperately clung to the hope that this was all a dream. But my gut told me it wasn't and that those fiery birds in the distance were very real.

"There's something else I should tell you," Tray said, glancing out the window at an approaching male in a suit that rivaled his own.

"Only something?" I countered, my tone lacking the

heat I desired. Because yeah, I still wasn't over our surroundings or those creepy gargoyles up the road.

"Well, many things," he admitted. "But I should probably warn you—my father is the Midnight Fae King."

The door opened before I had a chance to process that statement.

"Master Nacht," the male greeted, bowing. "So good to have you home, sir."

"It's only temporary, Clive," Tray replied. "Just giving Ella a brief tour."

"Of course, Master Nacht." The penguin suit stepped back a few feet, his arm gesturing for us to exit. He seemed normal enough. But so did Tray, and apparently he drank human blood.

I shivered at the thought.

Vampires.

Compulsion.

Dark magic.

Vine-like snakes.

Gargoyles.

What next? A hellhound, maybe?

"Ella," Tray murmured, his palm sliding down my arm in a gentle caress that should have left me cold but had the opposite impact entirely.

I had accused him of using compulsion on the dance floor earlier, but we both knew it was a lie. My body seemed to react to his as if we belonged together. A terrifying thought considering everything I'd learned tonight.

Although, perhaps not. I was half-fae, according to Tray. Which raised a myriad of questions.

Ones I doubted would all be answered tonight.

Which was good because I probably couldn't handle those details on top of everything else.

Sliding my feet back into my stilettos, I climbed out of the limo and stared up at the imposing black marble exterior. *Uh, hello, Dracula. I'm Ella. Nice to meet you. Please don't eat me.*

Tray slipped into the night behind me, the heat of his body the only indication he'd moved. His palm pressed to the small of my back, the touch tentative. I should push him away, but I refrained. It would only worsen the situation.

Clive disappeared through a grand set of doors at the front of the mansion, leaving the wood planks slightly ajar to signal his intention for us to follow. Or maybe he lurked on the other side, awaiting our approach so he could open the doors with a flourish.

I frowned. *Who even welcomes guests at this hour? And why are all the lights on?* It had to be well after midnight, maybe even later. But the gothic home was lit up like it was midday inside.

"What now?" I wondered out loud.

"Now I'll introduce you to my parents and my brother, Kols, if he's around." Tray gave me a little nudge, indicating he wanted me to walk.

"Your parents," I repeated. "Who are, like, uh, royalty?" *Oh, by the way, my father is the Midnight Fae King. And vampires are real. Welcome home, Ella!* I nearly laughed out loud at the ludicrous nature of my thoughts, but here we were, walking up the cobblestone drive toward Count Dracula's mansion.

Awesome.

"Yeah, as are you," he replied. "As I said, your mother was of the royal line, just a different family."

I stopped walking. "Does that mean we're like cousins?" Because that would be wrong on so many levels.

He snorted. "No. Not at all. Think of the royal lines like you would the famous family names in Darlington. None of them are related, but they run in the same circles. Similar concept, only we base our royalty on the power in our veins, not how much wealth we keep in our accounts."

"And you think I have magic." He'd mentioned it in the limo, that he thought I was blocking them because of my "emotional armor."

"I know you do, Ella." He shifted to stand in front of me, his hands falling to my hips. "Your mother's family is notoriously powerful. While her leaving our world wasn't exactly celebrated, she still maintained her access to the dark arts. And that gift should have passed to you."

"What do you mean by 'her leaving wasn't exactly celebrated'?"

A hint of unease darkened his gaze. "Those of the royal lines tend to have their futures designated for them. Your mother chose not to follow the path outlined by the Council, which created some tension."

"I thought you said human relationships happen because of the whole blood-drinking thing."

"They happen, yes, but that doesn't mean the relationships are well respected by our kind. And a royal declining an intended arrangement over a mortal affair is particularly rare. Your mother was fortunate that her father's position superseded the other family, or she'd have been forced to return."

Uh, that entire statement was rife with political red tape. What I gathered was that my mother came from an influential fae family that helped her break the rules for my father. As that all led to my creation, I couldn't exactly comment negatively on the arrangement.

But I also didn't fully understand it.

Tray cupped my cheek, tilting my head back to hold his gaze as he moved into my personal space. "There's a lot I need to explain, Ella. But I don't want to overwhelm you."

"Too late," I muttered.

His lips curled into a smirk. "Well, you didn't exactly leave me with any other choice. You were about to run and never look back."

"Correction, I wasn't about to run; I *was* running."

"But I caught you."

"And abducted me and forced me into a fae world," I finished for him. "Yeah, not sure that's adding points in your favor, Nacht."

"Yeah, I know," he agreed. "I've played this game entirely wrong."

"And that was your first error," I told him. "Considering my life a game makes you no better than anyone else."

"I don't consider your life a game, sweetheart." His gaze burned with an intensity that caused my heart to skip a beat. "Those bastard humans in Darlington created the game, but I failed to master my strategy despite my careful planning. I thought by befriending them and joining the inner circle, I could move them around like the pawns they are. But that bitch Ryan one-upped me, something she'll pay dearly for at some point."

"I…" I swallowed. "I don't know what to say to that." His sincerity had knocked the wit right out of me. There wasn't a single smart-ass reply I could make. So I went with a question instead. "What was your goal?"

He didn't miss a beat. "To watch you destroy them."

"How?"

"By dethroning those idiot stepsisters of yours and bringing Darlington royalty to their knees." His thumb traced my cheekbone. "I'd love to see you burn that shithole to the ground."

The embers flecking his obsidian irises told me he meant that literally, not figuratively. "You really want to avenge me."

"More than you'll ever know," he admitted. "What they've done to you is sick and disturbing, and the fact that those adults you call teachers do nothing to stop them only makes it worse. And don't get me started on your cunt of a stepmother." He physically shuddered. "Had I been allowed, I would have taken you to the Midnight Fae Realm far sooner. Unfortunately, you belonged in the human world until very recently."

"And now?" I prompted, startled by the end of his statement.

"You belong here, but the Council agreed to let you finish the human school year first."

My lips parted, words halting in my throat. *I belong here? With the vine-snakes and firebirds and creepy gargoyles? Uh, yeah, no.*

Nope. Not happening. Do not pass go. I—

"Trayton?" a female voice called from the doorway.

I glanced over his shoulder to see an elegantly poised female in a vibrant emerald dress waiting on the stoop. Her black eyes met mine, a hint of distaste coloring her flawless features.

Tray turned with a smile. "Hello, Mother."

Mother? I thought, my eyes widening. This woman couldn't be older than twenty-five, her porcelain skin nowhere near aging.

He walked into her open arms, kissing her cheek. "Apologies for our unexpected arrival. I wanted to show Ella our home." He stepped to her side and smiled. "Ella, this is my mother, Reba Nacht. Mother, this is Isabella Cinder."

"Cinder?" she repeated, arching a brow. "You mean Isabella Zorya, yes?"

Tray sighed. "We haven't reached that part of her familial history yet, Mother."

"That's my mother's maiden name," I said, frowning.

"It's your true name as well," Reba informed me, turning. "Come inside, Trayton. It's rude to keep the family waiting."

With that lovely invitation, she disappeared into the colossal home.

"Your mother adores me," I deadpanned.

Amusement flirted with Tray's features, giving him a younger appeal. "She's having a hard time accepting some of my choices, but she'll come around."

I arched a brow. "Choices? Like enrolling in Darlington Academy when you clearly don't need the high school degree?"

"Yeah, things like that." He held out his elbow. "Come on, Ella darling. I promise my parents won't bite."

"And you?" I countered, folding my arms. "Will you bite?"

He sauntered toward me, snagging me around the waist

with his arm before I could step away. "I'm going to do a lot more than bite you, sweetheart." He nipped at my bottom lip in a flash, leaving me hot and trembling against him.

How does he do *that?* I thought, livid with my innate reaction to him. *He's a vampire, for crying out loud!*

Yet I swayed in his arms like a damn damsel in distress.

"What is this pull you have over me?" I asked, breathless.

His lips curled. "I could ask you the same thing." He brushed his nose against mine. "Will you please come with me inside? I can't explain everything tonight, but at least you'll have an understanding of where I'm really from. Then we can discuss what comes next."

What comes next, I repeated to myself. What came next was me getting the hell out of here.

And then what? Head back to Darlington?

Yeah, because there was so much I enjoyed there. *Not.*

The last few years had all been about graduating so I could escape. To run as far away from Darlington as possible.

What could be farther than a fae realm?

Tray lifted his hand to massage the lines of my forehead. "Stop frowning at me."

"I'm not frowning at you." I was frowning at this bizarre situation. He'd taken me to a place where I could actually escape. A new life where I didn't have to worry about my stepsisters or Clarissa. A world with possibilities I'd never dreamed of. "What happens at Midnight Fae Academy?" Wasn't that what he called it? The college-like school his kind attended.

"We perfect our access to the dark arts."

"Right, you said that, but what does that mean?" An image of a wizard waving a wand around popped into my mind.

"There are a variety of dark-magic sects you can study, typically denoted by your bloodline. As a royal, you'll be enrolled in the Elite Program to learn more about the source of our power and how to control it." He drew his thumb across my lower lip. "You'll understand more once you ignite your gift."

"Which you think is blocked," I said, shivering from the soft caress against my mouth.

He nodded. "Yes."

"And you want to help me unblock it?"

"I do." He brushed a kiss against my cheek. "My mother is going to interrupt us again if we don't start moving."

"Was I supposed to curtsy?" I blurted out. "Is that why I offended her?" She was married to a king, right? *Wait...* "If your dad is..." My knees locked, realization slamming into my skull with the force of a freight train. "Holy crap." I should have deduced this when he first mentioned it. "That means you're a prince. And a future king?" I squeaked.

"Technically, that would be my role," a voice drawled from the dark. "But yes, my little brother is every bit the prince."

CHAPTER ELEVEN

TRAY

KOLS MATERIALIZED BESIDE US with a wicked grin, knowing how much I hated his *little brother* comment. "By two minutes," I muttered.

"Still makes me the future king and you a mere prince." He waggled his brows. "Unless you want to duel for it?"

The reference to our youth had me shaking my head. "We both know I don't want to win that challenge."

"So you continue to tell me," he replied, meeting Ella's wide gaze. "My brother here claims that every time I suggest a battle. Not only is he under the misconception that he'll win, but he also believes it means he'll inherit the throne." He zapped my side with a flicker of electricity, causing me to release Ella and send a volt back at him.

"This was an expensive suit," I complained, noting the

fraying material at my side.

"Aw, here, I'll fix that for you, little bro." He wiggled his fingers, weaving a hint of magic into the air that threaded the fabric back together.

"Will you two stop showing off and get in here?" my mother demanded from the doorway, her patience officially gone.

Ella appeared frozen, her eyes on the elemental flares lingering near my side.

"Two more minutes, Mom," I called to her. "Please."

She held my gaze for all of a second before throwing her arms up in the air in a gesture of defeat and retreating into the house.

"Dad has a meeting with Aswad tomorrow," Kols informed me. "It's put Mom on edge."

"I see that," I replied, my focus falling to Ella. "Are you okay with going inside, or would you prefer I take you home?" Because if that was her choice, I'd do it. Even if it meant staying up pretty much all night to make it happen. My compulsion had screwed with her sense of time, allowing her to think maybe an hour had passed since the dance. In reality, it was closer to five.

Fortunately, Midnight Fae were true to their name. We were night creatures, and it was only our equivalent of a late afternoon at the moment.

"You'll take me back?" she asked softly.

"If that's what you want, yes." I approached her again. However, I didn't touch her this time. "It would be wiser for us to stay, Ella. But I'll never force you to do something you don't want to do." Within reason, of course. She would eventually have to attend the Academy. Council rules and all that. Hence the importance of my job—to ensure that she *wanted* to enroll, thereby rendering the edict a moot point.

"I want to learn more," she said, her attention flickering between me and Kols before glancing up at our childhood home. "I want you to tell me about my mom."

I shared a look with my brother. We both knew that subject would upset our mother. She'd been best friends with Siobhan Zorya, once upon a time.

"I'll tell you whatever you want to know," I promised. "After we're done talking to my parents." It was a point I couldn't debate.

Fortunately, she accepted it with a nod. "Okay." She took a step forward, then paused. "Wait, you didn't clarify the curtsying thing."

Kols grinned. "I'd enjoy seeing that."

"Fuck off," I told him, focusing on her. "We don't follow human formalities."

"But we really should," my irritating twin put in. He feigned a bow and glanced up at her from his position, his golden eyes twinkling. "Hmm, yes, I do enjoy the view."

I rolled my eyes. "Stop flirting with my… *Ella*."

She gaped at me. "*Your* Ella?" She snorted. "We might be on your home turf, but I'm still very much in charge of myself, thank you very much."

Kols bit his lip to keep from laughing. I could practically hear him in my mind taunting, *Have fun taming this one, brother. She's a firecracker.*

Well, I'd rather be intended to her than the bitch our society had lined up for him.

Being a second born certainly came with certain benefits.

Such as my ability to choose anyone of the royal line to wed.

Poor Kols never had a choice.

And his sobering expression now told me he knew it, too.

He cleared his throat and righted his spine. "This custom suits," he said, holding out his hand for Ella. "I'm Kolstov. Family and friends—of which you are now—call me Kols."

"He's my twin," I added. "Clearly not identical."

"Yes, I was given the better looks," he said as Ella pressed her palm to his. He brought her wrist up to his mouth to bestow a kiss upon her flesh, his gaze glittering as he caught me narrowing my eyes at him in response.

Stop flirting with my betrothed, I told him with a look.

Just having some fun, his resulting smirk seemed to say.

"Twins," she mused, retracting her hand. "That's dangerous."

"Oh, you have no idea," Kols murmured. "Now come along, little Halfling. Our father is dying to meet you."

"Little Halfling?" she repeated, snorting. "All right, cocky prince, let's go."

He arched a brow. "Cocky prince?"

"What?" She blinked innocently. "I thought we were giving each other nicknames."

His lips curled. "Oh, I do like you." He glanced up at me. "Good choice, brother."

"Stop baiting her," I retorted, folding my arms.

"Me? Bait someone?" He pressed a hand to his chest, right over his heart. "Never."

Ella giggled and shook her head, causing me to frown. "Did you just laugh?"

"He's funny," she said, shrugging, her smile growing wider. "Charming, too. Why didn't you send him to Darlington? I may have liked him."

Ah, I see. "Now you're baiting me." I tsked. "Not a wise move, darling Ella. I'm your only ride home."

"Home." She scoffed. "That's not a point in your favor, Nacht."

"So I've lost two, then?" Because she said the same thing about my *abducting* her tonight.

"Oh, you've lost a hell of a lot more than that," she snapped, turning a conversational tone toward my brother. "Did you know he tried to drown me?"

"Drown you?" He gaped at me. "Why the hell would you try to drown your ma—"

"Enough," I growled, cutting him off. *She doesn't know yet,* I tried to tell him with my eyes. "Let's go inside," I said out loud, his brow furrowing in a way that told me we would be talking more about that little slip later.

Ella didn't seem to notice. She merely lifted a shoulder and flippantly said, "Sure. Why not?"

I knew better than to believe her nonchalant tone. Oh, she put on a strong front—likely born from years of having to protect her outward reactions—but beneath the surface, she boiled hot with questions. I could see it in the flare of her blue irises, her need to know more. Particularly about her mother.

Once we finished the family formalities, I'd do my best to assuage some of her curiosity. But a single night wouldn't be enough. We'd only just begun to scratch the surface.

The look my brother cast me now said he knew it, too.

And he didn't envy me at all. Not even a little.

CHAPTER TWELVE

☙ ELLA ☙

"WOW, THIS IS YOUR ROOM?" It was almost, well, *normal*. Dark, masculine colors, a desk, a sitting area with feathery throws, and a balcony overlooking the back of the estate. Oh, and a giant bed framed by two nightstands.

I ignored that part of Tray's quarters and gazed out at the double moon instead.

This was all so unreal.

Except his father had been just like every other dad I'd ever met. Apart from the whole *king* thing and the fact that he didn't look a day over twenty-five, just like his wife.

So not exactly typical, but not outwardly bizarre either.

I shook my head.

"What are you thinking about?" Tray asked, handing me a much-needed glass of water.

I chugged it before replying, my throat parched after what felt like hours of dehydration. When I finished, he plucked it from my hand and wandered over to the cooler in the corner to refill it.

"What's making you frown like that?" he pressed as he returned with my refilled cup.

I took another sip, sighing in contentment. *So refreshing.* I didn't bother asking if it was poisoned or possessed by magic. At this point, it no longer mattered. If he wanted to hurt me, he would have. Instead, he seemed rather intent on providing me with explanations. Which I was begrudgingly grateful for.

"Ella?"

I cleared my throat and met his concerned gaze. "I was thinking about Reba and Malik. They don't look old enough to be your parents."

"Ah, yeah, we age very differently from humankind. Our first twenty years or so are similar, then it sort of crawls for a few centuries. Most Midnight Fae live to be five or six hundred years old." He shrugged as if this wasn't mind-blowing information. "You'll notice it soon when you stop aging."

I felt like a fish out of water, gasping for breath. "I... You're saying..." I shook my head, clearing it so I could attempt a rational thought. "I'll live five or six hundred years?"

He nodded. "Give or take a few decades, yeah. It's pretty standard." He palmed the back of his neck, a glimmer of unease darkening his gaze. "We typically heal faster than mortals, and human disease doesn't impact us, but there are certain injuries we can't recover from."

"Like a head-on collision car accident," I said, understanding the discomfort in his features. "The police said she died instantly."

"Head trauma on that scale isn't something a fae can survive." He grimaced. "I'm sorry, Ella."

"For what? For my loss?" I couldn't help the bitterness

of my words. "Why does everyone say that? They should say what they really mean. *I pity you.*" Because that was what it was.

"I meant I was sorry for bringing up a sensitive topic," he clarified, his posture stiffening. "But I don't pity you, Isabella. Your life experiences are the core of your strengths. Feeling sorry for the losses you've endured would belittle the woman you've become, which would be unfair to both of us."

My annoyance cooled, his statement throwing me off guard.

Nothing this guy said or did added up to my expectations. Each time I made up my mind on something, he did the opposite. Almost as if he was born to taunt me.

"Now what are you thinking?" he asked, suspicion in his expression.

"You mean vampires can't read minds?"

He scoffed at that. "We're fae, sweetheart. Vampires are a legend."

"You drink blood," I reminded him.

"Sparingly." He folded his arms and leaned against the wall, leaving me to either stand in the open space of his lounge area or sit on the sofa.

I chose the sofa. As soon as my butt hit the cushion, a wave of exhaustion overwhelmed me. *Damn, what time is it anyway?* I wondered, glancing at the balcony beyond. The darkness hadn't let up since our arrival, suggesting it was maybe three or four in the morning. Assuming time worked the same here.

A bubble of a laugh caught in my throat. *Here*, I repeated to myself. *In Faeland.*

Magic lurked in every corner despite the modern decor of the home. Oh, there weren't any hellhounds or anything, just a sense of ethereal energy in the air. Flames had danced over Kols's fingertips on several occasions. At one point, he flicked one over to Tray that he'd deftly caught and smothered beneath a shadow of embers.

I'd watched in awe, every passing moment driving home the realness of this world. *I'm half-fae*, I thought for the thousandth time tonight. But I didn't *feel* gifted.

"What if my power never manifests?" I wondered out loud. "Do I go back to Darlington?"

"The better question is, how do we break the binds on your magic?" he countered, pushing off the wall to join me on the couch. He took up the opposite end, bracing his back against the arm of the sofa and drawing up one knee while leaving the opposite foot on the ground.

I mimicked his position so we could face each other. "Is it normal for a Halfling to have to 'break the binds'?"

"No. But nothing about your background is considered normal, Ella. You didn't even know you were half-fae until tonight. The few who exist all grew up with parents who knew how to help foster the growing powers."

"While my mother died when I was twelve," I said, thinking. "So why didn't my father say anything?" He'd died a few years later, shortly after marrying Clarissa.

"He likely didn't know." Tray shifted a little, his suit pants stretching across his thighs. My dress swallowed up half the couch, the skirt rustling with my every move.

How silly we probably appeared, sitting casually in our formal wear, talking about vampire-like fae.

"Your mother had to know her relationship with your father couldn't last," Tray continued, clearing his throat. "Mortals age much faster than we do. She'd still be in her early years of life when he passed. Thus, it's likely that whatever she felt was fleeting, but perhaps she stayed because of you."

I held up my hand to stop him. "My parents loved each other."

"I have no doubt they did, but humans love differently than fae do, Ella. Consider how easily your father moved on. If he had been a fae, that wouldn't have been possible."

My blood heated at the mention of my father moving on quickly. Because yes. Yes, he did. And it was a point that bothered me at the time and still irked me now.

How could a person who professes to love someone allow another woman into his life in less than a year? I was still mourning my mother's death the day he told me he was engaged to Clarissa. They'd wed soon after, gifting me two evil stepsisters and a stepmother who could hardly stand to look at me.

"*You have all your mother's features,*" she'd told me countless times. "*A pity, really. I never did understand what your father saw in her. I suppose it was kind of him to take her in off the streets, though.*"

I shuddered, recalling her scathing tone and the implications of her words. The wicked witch often claimed my mother was a miscreant who lived on my father's wealth and generosity. It took considerable effort not to point out the irony in her accusations. However, I bit my tongue because the last thing I wanted was to draw her attention to my mother or the finances she left behind in my name.

"We should get some rest," Tray said, standing. "I'll find you something more comfortable."

That wouldn't be hard. The satin gown, while beautiful, was not the most pleasant evening attire. Although, I probably could make a bed out of the puffy skirt.

Tray returned with a shirt and a pair of boxers and pointed to a door in the corner that led to a colossal bathroom decorated in ebony marble and silver fixtures. "Wow," I breathed, taking it all in. If Satan had a bathroom, it would look like this. Maybe with the addition of a fireplace.

Shaking my head, I set the clothes on the black countertop and untied the ribbon at the base of my spine. The corseted top had been laced up my back by the dress shop owner.

And I had no idea how to loosen it after undoing the bow.

I nibbled my lip, considering my options.

Scissors? I searched the drawers. *Nope.*

Try to tug it off? I danced around a few paces, gripping the satin and pulling without any success. Actually, it only seemed to make matters worse.

Light it on fire? Yeah, no, I valued my skin too much for that.

Which left me only one, very uncomfortable, idea. "Tray?" I called, looking upward and inwardly cursing my fate.

"Yeah?" he appeared in the doorway in a pair of gray pajama pants.

Nothing else.

I'd seen him shirtless earlier this week, but somehow he appeared even more sculpted and defined now. It had to be the lighting. Every divot on his chest and abdomen was clearly etched, as if he were made of stone. Only, he radiated heat, his skin a soft tan color that contrasted with my pale skin.

Definitely not very vampy, in terms of the legends.

But the sinful curve of his mouth certainly appeared wicked. "Ella?" he prompted, arching a reddish-brown eyebrow.

Uh, right. I'd called him in here.

With a shake of my head, I turned to give him my back. "Can you help extract me from this satin prison, please?" I met his gaze in the mirror. "Or, if you have something sharp, can I borrow it to cut myself out of this thing?"

He studied my gown as he considered. "Ruining such a beautiful dress would be a shame, Ella." He pushed off the door frame. "I'll loosen it for you."

I gripped the counter, my limbs locking as he tugged on the ribbon hanging off my tailbone. Warmth climbed up my neck, a result of his nearness and the woodsy aftershave taunting my senses. Why did he have to be so damn hot? Was it a fae thing? Because Kols was just as attractive as his brother. And their father also possessed a handsome charm, only heightened by his youthful appearance.

Vampires were notoriously good-looking, right? At least

in legend. So maybe all the fae were, too.

An entire world of sexy males with penchants for biting. Talk about a real-life wet dream. I swallowed and closed my eyes. *Clearly, I need a nap.* Because these types of thoughts were not okay or desired or even mildly appropriate. Especially with Tray standing so close to me.

Undressing me.

Caressing me.

I shivered as his breath kissed my exposed shoulder, the air between us seeming to thicken with every inhale. The fabric slowly loosened around my waist, the ribbon releasing a soft sifting sound as he unthreaded each loop. Goose bumps pebbled down my arms, my gloves long forgotten somewhere in the house. Or had I removed them in the limo? I couldn't remember, my focus entirely owned by the man behind me.

Fae, I mentally corrected. *But he certainly feels like a man.*

My stomach twisted, butterflies taking flight in my lower belly. His kiss earlier had consumed my mind, body, and soul, introducing me to sensations I'd only ever read about. But was it him or the magical powers he possessed? He'd promised it wasn't compulsion, yet it'd felt a lot like falling under the influence of a hypnotic drug.

Maybe I should kiss him once more to see if it happens again? I blinked open my eyes to gape at myself for the idiotic notion.

And found Tray watching me in the mirror, his gaze a smoldering black that stole the air from my lungs.

"It should be loose enough now," he whispered.

"Thanks," I managed to say, my throat dry.

He gave a nod and disappeared, leaving me to change. Or maybe to breathe. Both were tasks I needed to do.

I quickly exchanged the satin for the comfort of his cotton shirt and boxer shorts. Then I wasted some time in the bathroom finger-brushing my teeth and whatnot. My cheeks weren't as rosy in color by the time I returned to the bedroom, but my skin still felt hot all over. Which only intensified when I found him lounging on the couch with all those abs still on display.

He popped up onto his feet without a word, brushing by me as he wandered into the room I'd just left.

Right.

This wasn't awkward at all.

I eyed the bed against the wall, then took in the seating area. The sofa seemed safer. So I retrieved a few pillows and I was just putting them on the sofa when Tray returned. "I'll, uh, sleep here," I told him without looking at him.

"The hell you will," he retorted. "You'll take the bed. I'll be on the couch."

"It's your room," I reminded him. "And I'm perfectly fine with the sofa."

"You're right; this is my room. Which means you'll be taking the bed, Isabella. End of discussion."

Oh, no, he did not just try to command me. I spun around to face him, hands on my hips. "You can't make me sleep somewhere I don't want to sleep."

"Why do you have to be so difficult?" he asked, his expression and tone one of stark exasperation as he stalked toward me and pointed over my shoulder. "Just take the damn bed!"

"I don't want to sleep in your bed!" I shouted, right into his face.

"Why the hell not?" he demanded.

"Because I... It's the principle of the matter, Tray."

"The principle of the matter," he repeated, the heat of his torso practically melting the shirt from my own body. Or maybe it was my ire threatening to light the fabric on fire. "Fuck, woman, you drive me insane."

My eyebrows shot upward. "I drive *you* insane? You kidnapped me and brought me to a fae realm."

"Because you were being difficult. Wow, imagine that." He had the audacity to roll his eyes.

"Are you kidding? You told me to go fetch you a drink like a dog while you danced with Ryan. Right after kissing *me.* In front of the whole school. Excuse me for reacting accordingly."

"You *ran.*"

"Of course I did!" God, this guy was impossible. "Can you blame me? You chose Ryan over me."

"I did not."

"No? You sent me off on an errand, Trayton. So you could dance with *her,* of all people." Just thinking about it caused my blood to boil. My fists curled at my sides. "I'm not sleeping in your bed. In fact, I want a new room. Maybe Kols will let me sleep on *his* couch."

He growled, stepping into my personal space and wrapping his arm around my lower back to hold me in place. "Over my dead body."

"I'd happily arrange that," I said sweetly.

He snorted. "I just bet you would." He kept one arm around my back while his opposite hand came up to cradle my cheek—a rather tender move considering the anger vibrating off him in waves. "There's just one thing you're forgetting, Isabella Cinder."

"Yeah?" I grabbed his wrist, squeezing in warning. "And what's that?"

"You want me alive," he replied. "Because otherwise, I couldn't do this."

His mouth claimed mine before I could issue a retort. Not that I had one. Because holy crap, Trayton Nacht was kissing me. Again.

CHAPTER THIRTEEN

TRAY

ISABELLA CINDER DROVE ME CRAZY. I couldn't tell if I wanted to kill her or fuck her.

No.

That wasn't true.

Right now? I very much wanted to fuck her. Preferably against the wall, and hard. Because damn, she had a mouth on her. Content and quiet one moment, and biting my head off the next. Did I deserve it? Maybe. But not over the damn bed. I'd offered it to be a gentleman, and she'd turned that gesture around on me for no practical reason.

Insufferable female.

Oh, but she tasted minty and fresh and very much *mine*.

I tightened my grip around her as she melted into me. At least in this she submitted, her body recognizing mine on a level she would soon understand—intimately.

My tongue seduced hers, my palm sliding from her cheek to the back of her neck to better angle her head to receive my kiss. She moaned, the sound going straight to my already hard dick.

I walked her backward toward my bed, hoping like hell it didn't ignite our bickering. Or maybe I'd welcome it. There were worse activities than kissing this woman into submission.

She gave a little squeak when the back of her legs hit the mattress, but I swallowed her protest and grabbed her hips to lift her into the air. Another of those surprised little sounds fell from her lips as I picked her up. "Tray—"

I tossed her into the center of the bed and climbed over her before she could argue. "Shush, Isabella. We're done talking. All I want is to devour you." I took her mouth again, silencing whatever she'd been about to say.

A low groan vibrated her throat, causing me to smile.

Yes, darling, I thought. *Just like that.*

Her fingers threaded through my hair, holding me to her as she returned my kiss with a fierce one of her own. And damn if it didn't light my soul on fire for her.

Fuck.

This woman was going to kill me in the best way.

My palms slid up her sides, memorizing her svelte curves over the fabric of my shirt—which looked so damn hot on her that I wanted to rip it off. But I wouldn't push her. The way she shivered as my hands brushed the swell of her breasts confirmed all my suspicions about her innocence. Ella had hardly been touched. Not surprising given her last few years of hell.

Mmm, she would require a slow introduction.

I could handle that.

I trailed my lips across her jaw to her neck, then kissed the hollow of her throat before nibbling her racing pulse. She jolted beneath me, her body recognizing my darker desire. "Don't worry, little dove," I whispered, licking the slender column up to her ear. "I won't bite you."

Not because I didn't want to.

But because it would initiate our mating trial.

And she'd been through more than enough tonight.

"Tray," she whispered, arching into me in a needy way that made it *very* hard for me to behave.

I slid one of my thighs between hers to provide the pressure she unknowingly craved, my mouth returning to hers. The heat radiating from her core went straight through the fabric of our clothes, branding my skin and setting my blood on fire for her. I allowed the intensity to fuel our kiss, my tongue claiming hers.

She groaned.

I growled.

The sounds of our passion were a prelude to our future. Our souls already knew our fates, the bloodlines tied in a manner neither of us could deny. I felt it that day I met her, the stark yearning to claim her as mine.

Most Midnight Fae never experienced the instant connection, our matings arranged by the Council or through familial pairings. Fortunately, my intended came from an acceptable bloodline even with her Halfling heritage tainting her fae essence.

Oh, there was still so much to explain to her.

So much to *teach* her.

And not just in the bedroom.

Although, I wouldn't mind starting there.

I skimmed my hands up her sides again, this time beneath the shirt. Her overheated skin felt heavenly against my palms. My thigh flexed in time with her eager movements, her senses completely lost to the lust-driven cloud consuming us.

Instinct told me I could take anything I wanted from her like this, her body utterly mine in these precious moments.

Which meant I needed to proceed carefully, to maintain and *earn* her trust.

She raked her nails down my spine, grabbing my ass to

pull me impossibly closer, her little mewls of satisfaction music to my ears.

This, I could give her.

But nothing more.

Not until she could think clearly and properly consent.

I nipped her jaw, sucked the tender point between her neck and her shoulder, and allowed my fingers to wander dangerously close to her fleshier curves. Her nipples were hard through the thin fabric of the shirt, calling for my touch, but that earlier tremble remained at the forefront of my mind.

Not yet, I thought. *But soon.*

Ella whimpered, her pleasure cresting between her legs. I felt it in the dampness bleeding into my pants. My tongue longed for a taste, her arousal permeating the air around us and seducing my senses.

"You're killing me," I admitted softly, practically panting against her neck.

Her fingers returned to my hair, tugging me up to kiss her again, her mouth wild against mine.

She'd accuse me of compelling her again.

But I wasn't.

It was her inner fae fighting to come out, to claim what she recognized as hers.

Explaining that was going to be a nightmare.

Or maybe she'd surprise me and accept it. She'd certainly handled everything else somewhat well so far.

Ella pushed into my thigh on a sharp thrust, her back bowing off the bed as a cry spilled from her beautiful lips.

"Gorgeous," I marveled out loud, admiring her as she fell apart beneath me.

Golden hair fanned against my pillows.

Rosy cheeks.

A swollen mouth designed for sin.

My cock ached, desperate to play, but I swallowed the urge and nuzzled her throat instead, to help bring her down from her high. She released a long breath, her grip loosening in my hair.

And then she stiffened.

Yeah, I expected that, I thought, mentally sighing.

"Wh-what did you just do to me?" she stammered, her heart racing a mile a minute.

"Exactly what I said I would," I replied, bracing myself on my elbows—my forearms resting on the mattress along either side of her head. If she wanted to escape, she'd have one hell of a fight.

"I... I don't..." She blinked, her blue eyes an intoxicating mix of pleasure and confusion.

"I devoured you, sweetheart." I smiled. "And you enjoyed it."

"You com—"

"I did not compel you," I interjected, cutting off the accusation before she could give it a voice. "I kissed you. And those swollen lips of yours are proof that you more than kissed me back. Compulsion alters perception, Isabella. And you were not only aware but also complicit throughout all of that, including your orgasm."

She stared at me for a long second. "Yeah, I was going to say you completely blew my mind, but okay."

I narrowed my gaze. "While I know I did, I doubt that's what you were going to say."

"Well, you'll never know now since you so rudely interrupted me." She placed her hands on my shoulders, shoving upward. "Move."

I didn't budge. "No." I pressed my lips to the edge of her mouth to soften my refusal and added, "I'm sorry, Ella." I skimmed my nose across her cheek to kiss her jaw. "Forgive me, please?" I didn't want to ruin the moment, not when we were so close to finally understanding each other.

She tugged on my hair, yanking my head back to meet her gaze, her expression scrutinizing. "I can't tell if you're poking fun at me or if you actually mean that."

Sighing, I rolled off her and onto my back beside her. My thigh tingled with the reminder of her arousal, my dick still hard as a fucking rock inside my pants. But my mind... my mind was tired. It'd been a long day, and we really needed to get some rest.

"Can I share the bed with you?" I asked her softly, too exhausted to bicker anymore. "I promise to keep my hands to myself. I'll even sleep on top of the sheets."

I didn't look at her while I spoke, my focus on the high ceiling above. Mostly because I didn't want to see her expression. If she went into another rant about the sleeping arrangements, I'd go sleep on Kols's couch or something.

Silence.

Of course.

All right, well, clearly, she wanted space. "Okay, I can take a hint," I said, sitting up. "It's been an eventful evening, and all of this is a lot to take in. I'm going to go hang out with Kols. We need to catch up anyway." Not true. But I suspect Ella would argue if she knew I was giving up my room for her. Wasn't that what set her off earlier? My offering my bed?

I nearly snorted. *Impossible female.*

Her hand snagged my wrist before I could leave the bed, her grip surprisingly strong. "Stay," she said, clearing her throat. "I mean please. Please stay."

My eyebrows shot upward. *Did she just say something mildly polite?* I almost uttered the words out loud but thought better of it. Because those would spike another argument. Instead, I lay back down with a softly spoken "Okay."

A calm energy settled between us, one I welcomed with a yawn.

Ella rotated on her side, facing me. "Why did you dance with Ryan?" Her whisper of a voice pulled my focus toward her, my eyes meeting hers as I remained on my back beside her.

"Because I wanted to have a word with her regarding her unwelcome interruption," I admitted. "Your stepsisters want me to make you fall in love with me so I can break you publicly in front of the school. I pointed out to her that her intrusion was counterproductive to the goal."

Ella gaped at me. "*What?*"

"Yeah, your stepsisters are evil incarnate. Hence the reason I want them destroyed." I rolled my head back onto the pillow again, my gaze flickering up to the ceiling once more. "My thought is that we'll date for a few months, while secretly working on a way to bring them all down. Then, right about when Ryan expects me to shatter your heart, we'll demolish her instead."

Ryan and Carmen didn't have hearts, so playing them in a similar manner wouldn't work.

"I think it's their social status we need to dismantle," I added, thinking out loud. "We'll need to decide if Clarissa should burn with them."

Ella popped up onto her elbow, her blue eyes bright as she stared down at me. "You're serious."

"Yeah. I think I've mentioned this idea a few times."

"You really want me to get revenge on them."

"Of course I do." My brow furrowed. "What I want to know is, why don't you want revenge? Those bitches have put you through hell and back. Dash and Charlie are no better. Why do you allow it? Why don't you fight back?"

"Because fighting back only brings on more attention. I learned a long time ago that ignoring them affords me more peace."

"Peace," I repeated, snorting. "Was this week peaceful for you? With Charlie pestering you every morning in English class, the two idiots wanting to drown you in the pool, and then that circus tonight at the dance?"

"Well, it was more eventful than normal, thanks to a new student showing up," she drawled.

"Come on, Ella. Be serious for a moment. Even had I not shown up, those two idiots would have pestered you. And who knows what your stepsisters would have done had I not offered the distraction of a new game."

"Wait, *you* suggested the whole breaking-my-heart thing?"

"More like I steered Ryan into the idea," I clarified. "It gave me an excuse to spend time with you, while also pretending to be on their team. Win-win."

She scoffed at that. "Being on their team isn't a win."

"It is when you want to take the bastards down," I countered, going onto my elbow to mimic her pose. "Think about it, Ella. If they believe I'm on their side, they'll let down their guard around me and give us ways to infiltrate their circle and destroy them from the inside. It's a brilliant plan."

"Seriously, why are you wasting your time on this?" she demanded. "They're a bunch of high school humans. Seems pretty insignificant when compared to all this." She gestured with a hand around my room, but I understood what she meant—the Midnight Fae Realm.

"Something they've done has hindered your access to your powers." I reached across the space between us to palm her cheek. "I take that offense very seriously. As should you, Ella. You've spent years crafting impenetrable walls to hide from their torment, and I suspect that's part of the block on your inner fae."

She bit her cheek, then shook her head slowly. "I just don't see how exacting revenge will help me in the long run."

"Maybe it won't help you, but it'll help the next person they bully. And it's very likely that whoever their next target is won't be nearly as strong as you." Actually, I could guarantee it. Ella had endured enough torment to last a lifetime. It strengthened her in ways that would benefit her in the Midnight Fae Realm, assuming we could figure out how to unlock her gifts.

"I've never thought about that," she said quietly, lying down on her side once more, facing me. I copied the motion, my hand sliding to her neck. "I've always focused on escaping, not what would come next for them."

"They've existed in a world where they can do whatever they want to whomever they want, without punishment. I can only imagine the wickedness in their future. It won't be pleasant for whomever they target."

"Unless we find a way to teach them a lesson."

Oh, I wanted to do more than that. They didn't deserve a mere lesson, but a complete life change—one that put them in their own personal purgatories. However, I would follow Ella's lead in this. She could decide the level of punishment.

"There are still several months left of the school year," I murmured. "The longer it takes for our relationship to develop, the more time we'll have to plot against the supposed royalty of Darlington. Plus, in the interim, I can teach you more about the Midnight Fae and our Academy, and we can explore the binds on your abilities."

"So you're planning to come back to high school with me," she said, a wry note in her voice. "Sounds like you're punishing yourself."

I smirked. "Trust me, I'm not."

"Uh-huh." Her eyes twinkled. "You're saying you enjoy being my little fairy god—uh, well, no. Not godfather." She scrunched her brow. "I guess a guardian angel, except not."

"I'm a fae, not a fairy," I corrected. "And I'm definitely not an angel."

"It's from a fairy tale," she said. "You know, the fairy godmother? Helps the chick get ready for the ball? You pretty much did that tonight. Although, you failed to get me back by midnight." Her eyes widened. "No, you brought me to the Midnight Fae Realm. Holy crap, I'm..." She shook her head. "Yeah, never mind. I need to sleep now."

Given all the gibberish she'd just spouted at me, I couldn't agree more. "Yeah, that's a good idea."

She huffed a delirious little laugh and rolled around in the blankets, creating an adorable little nest on her side of the bed. I loved how small and protected she appeared, engulfed by satin and cotton. She closed her eyes, her head burrowing into the pillow.

I sent a spark of magic to the lights, dimming them to a

dusk-like glow. The blackout shades would slide down in about an hour. Something told me she'd be too exhausted to notice.

"Tray?" she murmured.

I glanced at her, but her eyes were still closed. "Yeah?"

"You can sleep under the sheets."

CHAPTER FOURTEEN

✿ ELLA ✿

MY STEPMOTHER DIDN'T NOTICE MY ABSENCE. Or maybe she did and just didn't care. All my chores were done before school this morning, which seemed to be her only concern in terms of my existence.

I blew a stray strand of hair out of my face and waited for my English class to begin.

It was surreal sitting here after everything I'd learned over the weekend.

Fae are real.

Tray drinks blood.

Tray kisses like a god.

I shivered at the memory of his hands roaming up and down my sides and the way his thigh had lodged between mine as I pressed up against him. My experience wasn't vast.

Dash had kissed me a few times, pawed at my boobs outside my clothes, and grabbed my ass on several occasions. Nothing exciting and certainly not like what Tray had done to me.

"Daydreaming about me, dove?" Tray asked as he sauntered toward the back of the classroom. He'd been busy shooting the shit with Charlie near the classroom door—a task I was sure he'd despised, yet somehow pulled off with an easy smile the whole time.

I batted my eyelashes up at Tray as he stopped in front of me. "I am, actually. I just stabbed you through the heart and it was glorious."

A few students chuckled around us, the human sheep always eavesdropping.

"You wound me, Cindersoot," he drawled, collapsing into his chair.

"If only it were real," I returned.

We'd decided our best play was to feign hatred and animosity toward each other after what went down at Homecoming. Ryan would love the idea that Tray had to work to earn my heart—because breaking it in the end would be all the sweeter.

"Oh, it was real," he replied, loud enough for everyone to hear. "Every lick, moan, and kiss, darling dove."

I rolled my eyes. "Yeah, you kissed me at the dance. Big deal."

"You seemed to think so." His irises smoldered as he looked me over. "I bet you'd kiss me again under the right circumstances."

My lips twitched because, yeah, I'd totally let him kiss me again under pretty much any circumstance. But out loud I replied, "Sure. At night. While you're dreaming."

He winked at me. "We'll be doing a lot more than kissing in my dreams, dove."

"And you'll be endlessly dying in mine, dick."

Professor Montgomery chose that moment to enter, her focus immediately falling on me. "Miss Cinder, language!"

"This project you've assigned is impossible, Professor Montgomery," Tray said, wasting no time. "She won't even agree to meet with me for the project despite my offering endless hours for the interview."

I coughed out a laugh. "Excuse me, but I recall you saying you were busy every night last week."

"I don't recall any such claim," he replied, his attention on the teacher. "How am I supposed to finish my first assignment with a partner who refuses to work with me?"

She set her bag on her desk, her expression one that said she truly hated Mondays. Or maybe it was her students she despised. Or just us.

"Is that true, Miss Cinder?" she demanded. "Are you refusing to be accommodating to our new student?"

"I've witnessed it firsthand," Charlie put in unhelpfully. "Tray asked her nicely last week to spend time after school for an hour, and she told him to go to hell. Apologies for the language."

Tray lifted a shoulder, neither confirming nor denying the accusation.

I knew this was all part of our ploy, but *Jesus*. Could he have chosen a different avenue for our bickering? One that didn't impact my grade point average.

"I did no such thing," I stated truthfully. "He demanded I go to Homecoming with him to work on our project." Yeah, just saying that out loud, I heard how ridiculous it sounded. And Montgomery's expression said she'd heard it, too.

"Well, since both of you seem unable to accommodate the other, how about a week of after-school detention to work out your differences and your project?" she suggested, arching a brow.

Shit.

Clarissa was not going to like that. Not one bit.

I never received detention. Ever.

"Great, I'm glad that's settled," Professor Montgomery said, not giving us time to argue. "I'll see you both promptly after last period. Bring your notebooks."

Awesome, I thought with a mental huff. *Thanks, Tray.*

This plan of his had better be worth it. Because if I just accepted detention for no benefit whatsoever, he'd have hell to pay.

I waited impatiently for Montgomery to carry out her lecture, desperately wanting to pull Tray aside to demand an explanation. But as soon as the bell rang, he disappeared with the other students into the hallway and left me glaring after him.

Yeah, that went well.

I continued through my next few classes, irritated and confused and decidedly pissed off. So when Tray yanked me into a vacant classroom just before lunch, I rounded on him. "What the hell are you doing?" I demanded.

"This." He grabbed my face between his palms and pushed me up against the wall beside the locked door, his mouth claiming mine.

I melted on instinct, my insides turning to mush.

Because Tray's lips? They were heaven.

My fingers wove through his hair, my body arching into his, needing to feel the heat of his body against every inch of my own. He was becoming my addiction—wrong and oh-so right. I shouldn't enjoy this, should demand he explain the detention plan, but I couldn't get a word in with his tongue in my mouth.

By the time he released me, I was panting in the best way, my skin overheated and tight.

"You look gorgeous," he whispered, running his nose across my cheekbone. "I'll see you in swim class."

"Wait." I caught his wrist before he could leave, tugging him back. "Why detention?"

"Gives us an excuse to see each other. Don't worry; I plan to enchant Montgomery so we can talk freely." He pressed his lips to my temple. "Then I'll come by your place after to help with anything you need, as I'm sure the step-monster will have a list of overdue chores for you."

When he said things like this, it became far too evident that he knew me better than I knew him. And considering we just met a week ago, that shouldn't be the case. "How do you know that about Clarissa?"

"Because the Council has kept tabs on you for years, Ella. I was given an entire file about you before arriving." He palmed my cheek. "I need to get to lunch. We'll talk more later."

* * *

"I WANT TO SEE THE FILE" were my first words after Tray knocked Montgomery out with a spell. She snored softly from her position at the desk, her head tipped back in a way that would leave her with a neck cramp later. Part of me wanted to go readjust her position. Then I recalled how quickly she'd acted earlier in assigning me detention when she was the reason I had to work with Tray to begin with.

Yeah, she more than deserved a neck cramp.

"Of course," Tray said in response to my demand to see the file. "I'll bring it over tonight."

I blinked. "You will?"

He shrugged. "I'll answer whatever you want to know, Ella. And that includes sharing the details I have on your past."

"Oh." For some reason, I'd expected him to fight me on this. "Er, thanks." I flipped open my notebook, then closed it. "So what are we doing now?" Because interviewing him seemed frivolous at this point. Although, I would need some details for the assignment. "Do you have a file on your cover for the Human Realm?"

"I have some legal documents, if you want to see them. But as far as everyone knows, I moved here to live with my recluse of an uncle while my parents gallivant around the world on a yearlong adventure. They just couldn't wait until I graduated." He lifted a shoulder. "Pretty simple, really. My father is a finance firm investor from London, and my mother is a debutante from Chicago. They own FAE Enterprises. Which, if you google it, is a real company. And yes, my parents actually do own it. But they have humans who oversee the board."

"Wait, why?"

"Because we're Midnight Fae, darling. We commonly interact with mortals."

"To feed," I translated.

He dipped his chin in affirmation. "Yes. Many of my kind have covers in the Human Realm. It helps explain our constant appearances. But we vary our interests throughout the world, so that way our feeding is spread out as well. My father has dominion over the United Kingdom and the East Coast of the United States. Anyone from a royal line—which we call Elite Magic—can feed in those areas. Aswad—a ruling monarch of the necromancy side—owns the southern United States. Thus, anyone with Death Magic can play down there, and so on."

There was a lot of information in that statement.

So much so that I didn't know where to start.

"Uh, okay." I cleared my throat. "There are different types of magic within the Midnight Fae?" That seemed a reasonable place to begin.

He nodded. "There are several. Elite Magic, Death Magic, Blood Magic, Warrior Magic, and Malefic Magic are the primary sects. The Academy is actually divided based on those sections. I'll reside on the Elite Quad with Kols in the fall. It's also where you'll live, if you join us."

"At the Academy, you mean."

Another nod.

"Because my mom was a royal?" I asked, clarifying.

"She was an Elite Magic user, yes." He leaned his elbows on the desk, his seat directly across from mine. "Our Midnight Fae line is closest to the heart of our darker element. It's why we're considered Elite—we harbor the most power of all our kind. But the other sects have their own powers and abilities. Death Magic, for example, is what humans call necromancy."

"They call upon the dead," I whispered, shivering.

"Among other things, yeah." He brushed his fingers through his hair, sighing. "There's a lot for me to explain, but what's most important is for us to tap into your gifts."

"Assuming I have them."

"You do." Tray sounded certain, as if there couldn't possibly be an alternative. "Give me your hand. I want to show you something."

"Uh, okay." I obliged, curious.

He clasped my wrist with one hand while using his finger of the other to draw a line of tingling energy across the fleshy surface of my palm. I quivered at the heated embers racing across my skin, the blue sparks dancing in a hypnotic pattern.

"That's how I know," he murmured, his lips tugging at the corner. "My magic recognizes you as a conduit—which marks you as a fae."

"What would that do on a human?"

Tray lifted a shoulder. "It'd burn them."

I snatched my hand back. "You did that knowing it might hurt me?"

He chuckled. "I did that knowing it *wouldn't* hurt you, El. You're a Halfling. I sensed it in you the night we met, and it's still very much there. We just need to figure out why your talent is hiding and break it free."

"Okay, first, you and your nicknames are just..." I trailed off, shaking my head. *Isabella. Ella. El. Dove. Darling. Sweetheart. Ugh.* "And second, how do you propose we do that, dear Fairy Guardian?"

"Fairy Guardian?" he repeated.

"Would you prefer I call you Mr. Nicknames?" I offered. "Because I can roll with that as well."

He snorted. "Tray is fine."

"As is Ella."

He scratched his jaw, considering. "What about Ella Bella?"

"How about no?" I countered.

His lips curled. "You're making me want to kiss you again, *Ella*."

"We're supposed to be learning right now, *Tray*."

"Oh, it would definitely be a learning experience. Trust me."

I lifted my eyes heavenward. "We are never going to find my hidden fae talents if all you want to do is make out with me."

"On the contrary, I might be able to ignite them with a few thorough orgasms. Shall we test the theory and find out?"

I gave him a look. "Seriously, fae or human, all boys think about is sex."

"I'm a man, not a boy," he clarified. "And what's wrong with that? Sex is fun."

Meaning he was experienced.

Which, yeah, I sort of knew that based on the way he kissed. But knowing he'd fooled around before had my stomach cramping for a multitude of reasons.

Not only had he been with other girls, but he'd also have expectations.

Expectations I might not be able to live up to with my lack of sexual know-how.

Why am I even thinking about this?

We had far more important things to focus on. Like my powers. And revenge. And my uncertain future.

"Tell me more about Midnight Fae Academy," I said, needing a new topic.

Fortunately, he conceded and dropped the other one.

Thirty minutes later, I had a thorough understanding of the Academy. "So it's like a university for fae." He'd mentioned dorms, finals, course schedules, professors, and even intramural sports. "Except there's only one available, not a whole smorgasbord of choices."

"It's also not voluntary," he added. "All Midnight Fae from twenty to twenty-four years old are mandated to attend."

"Oh." That sounded a bit ominous. "Even Halflings?"

"Yes."

"So I won't have a choice?"

"Not without Council intervention, no." He cleared his throat. "But it's where you belong, Ella. Your aging will begin to slow in the next year or so, and when your powers finally manifest, you'll want to be around your own kind for training. There's no reason *not* to enroll."

"Unless I want to go to a human university," I pointed out, folding my arms and leaning back into my chair.

"Sure, but why would you do that?"

"Maybe I want to at least have the choice," I countered.

He gave me a look that said he knew I was just being difficult. My life goal was to escape, and he'd offered me the opportunity on a pedestal. Why would I reject it?

"Okay, let's say I go." I held up my hand to stop him from commenting on my loose agreement. "What if I can't access my powers? How will that impact my enrollment?"

"It'll prove problematic," he confirmed. "Which is why we're going to focus on releasing them."

CHAPTER FIFTEEN

TRAY

One Month Later

I SAT IN MY USUAL BOOTH, my brother across from me, enjoying a bucket of his favorite flavor of wings. But I couldn't stomach mine. "I've tried everything, Kols. Nothing is working."

We'd attempted all the tricks I'd learned as a kid, even a few I'd read about in a variety of dark-magic books. With each trial, Ella grew more agitated, her belief in her lack of powers growing by the day.

But I knew they were in her somewhere.

I just couldn't figure out the key to unlocking them.

Kols wiped off his hands with a napkin, his manners as formal as ever despite the messy meal. "I'm telling you, T.

Just bite her."

Flames flickered across my hands on the table, my patience at an all-time low. "That's your solution to everything, isn't it?"

"Have you tried it?" he countered.

"Of course not. It'll initiate the mating bond."

Oh, fae could bite humans as often as they desired without any side effects—assuming they didn't drink too much, of course. But biting a fae with a desirable bloodline? Yeah, that created an eternal promise, one the females of our species were bound to regardless of their willingness.

I didn't want to do that to Ella.

Even if the Council required it.

"You're going to have to bite her eventually," Kols pointed out. "So why not start now and see what happens?"

"Sure. The second you bite Emelyn, I'll bite Ella."

He scowled. "The two are not mutually exclusive."

I arched a brow. "So you're saying you don't want to bite Emelyn yet?"

"Fuck you. You know I don't." He shuddered, the mention of his *betrothed* always a surefire way to sour his mood.

Our parents had designated the match over a decade ago, forcing our families to bond throughout the years.

Emelyn Jyn made Ryan look like a tender princess.

"It's different for you and Ella," Kols added. "You actually *like* your chosen mate."

My lips curled. "Oh, I more than like her." Keeping my hands off her had been quite the challenge these last few weeks.

I wanted to give her time to learn to trust me and to adjust to her new reality. The way she kissed me grew increasingly eager, confirming our mutually deepening feelings.

But we weren't quite there yet.

Unlocking her power seemed to be the key.

Kols took a long sip of his water and set it to the side.

"All right, so you think her gifts are wrapped up in this abusive childhood, right?"

I nodded.

"Why not take one or two of those obstacles down and see what happens," he suggested. "Maybe it'll loosen her up a little."

It was something to consider. I just didn't know how to do that without ruining the long-term game.

We had the entire Darlington crew right where we wanted them—believing I was her new tormentor and suitor. Ryan and Carmen were in heaven watching our back-and-forth play, wondering how I would pull this off in the long run.

It meant I had to talk to them frequently.

But at least it kept Ella safe from their torment.

"I'll consider that option," I eventually replied, meaning it. We could always take down Dash or Charlie first, but it would have to be subtle.

"I stand by option number one, T. Bite her."

With a theatrical sigh, I pulled out my wallet to toss some bills on the table. "Right, well, you've been very helpful," I drawled, standing.

He waggled his brows. "Feeling thirsty?"

Yes. I hadn't fed my darker urges enough over the last month and needed to change that tonight. "What gave me away?" I asked. "The eyes?"

"And your mood." He added some money to the table and stood as well. "Actually, I could use a bite. So I'll join you."

"Suit yourself. I was just going to a local bar."

"I have a much better location in mind," he replied. "Come with me, little brother. I know just what you need."

"I'm taller than you," I pointed out, waving at Belinda behind the bar before following Kols outside. "And I don't want to get laid." Well, I did, but not by a random chick. I wanted Ella and only Ella.

"Well, you might not want to, but I do." He led me to a

fancy sports car—one he'd borrowed from the garage of the Darlington residence. We kept it as a base for the family, which was why I'd taken up residence for school purposes. "You can feed without fucking, and I'll do it the preferred way."

I shook my head, sliding into the passenger seat beside him. Refusing him would be a moot point. He'd just talk me into heading out with him.

"You could invite your Ella to join us," he suggested, causing my blood to warm.

"And have her watch me feed from another woman? I'd rather fuck a gargoyle."

He grimaced. "Ouch, dude."

"Truth, *dude*," I returned.

Kols started the car, then paused, his expression darkening. "Actually, we should bring her."

"I just said—"

"Yeah, I heard you, but think about it for a second. She can't access her powers, right? Why do we drink human blood?"

Holy shit, I thought, my eyebrows lifting. "Why the hell didn't I think of that?"

"Because you're too busy making out with her to think straight. Not that I blame you. She's gorgeous."

"Yeah, she's also mine," I reminded him. "So don't get any ideas."

"Not entirely, T. You haven't bitten her yet," he mused, tapping his jaw.

"Careful, K," I cautioned. "I would hate to have to tell our father how his preferred heir died while in the Human Realm."

He chuckled, totally unfazed by my very real threat. "Call your intended. Invite her out to play so we can test our theory."

Yeah, this would be a fun conversation.

Let's drink blood together, baby.

Yes, please!

Like that would happen.

With a barely suppressed sigh, I dialed her number—I'd gifted her a phone shortly after our trip to the Midnight Fae Realm—and prepared for the worst.

* * *

ELLA AGREED TO THE PLAN. And not after several rounds of bickering over the issue, she'd accepted the idea immediately.

Apparently, she was as desperate as I was to figure out her missing link.

I glanced at her, admiring the way her fitted black dress cut off at the middle of her thighs. Similar to Homecoming, she hadn't owned anything club-worthy. So we'd made a stop on our way to the portal and she'd chosen this sexy little number. Her blonde hair was tied up in a messy bun, her face devoid of makeup, and a pair of black heels on her slender feet.

Perfection.

Beautiful.

Mine.

I squeezed her hand and brought her wrist to my lips.

I leaned down to ask, "You okay, El?" *El* had become my preferred nickname for her. While she'd protested it at first, her cheeks seemed to redden every time I said it now. Like she enjoyed me having a special name just for her.

"I'm still reeling from the portal experience," she admitted against my ear, the music vibrating the club around us. "I can't believe one exists in the Darlington Library."

"We have them all over," I informed her. "All the fae use them, not just Midnight Fae." Like a network of teleporters, but they required unique codes to reach different realms and locations. If a human stumbled upon one, it would function like a standard elevator within the building. However, enter a specific code in the pad, and it took the rider to a whole new world of fun.

In our case, we ventured off to London since it was several hours ahead and prime nightclub hour for a Friday night.

She glanced around, her cocktail forgotten on the tall table before us. Her gaze fell on my brother dancing near the edge of the floor with a cute little brunette. She had her arms draped around his neck, pushing her breasts into his chest in a clear offer. While he grinned down at her, I caught the tightening of his jaw.

He wanted a challenge, not an easy conquest.

So he might only feed tonight after all.

"Tray?" Ella placed her palm on my chest and pressed her lips to my ear again. "You're going to have to teach me how to, uh, do this."

I released her hand to wrap my arm around her back and tug her into my side. "Let's watch Kols," I said into her ear.

"No." She curled into me and gripped the lapel of my blazer. "I want *you* to show me."

I gaped at her. "You want to watch me with another woman?"

She scowled. "What? *No.*" Her emphatic response left me frowning.

"Then what, Ella?"

"Bite me," she said. "I want to know how it feels and all that. And also to, uh, see how you do it. Well, to understand it. Like, do the teeth sharpen?" Her eyes widened a little. "Do you have fangs?"

I chuckled, despite the weight pressing down on my chest. "No, El. No fangs."

Her relieved expression only increased my amusement. "Well, that's good, then. So you'll show me?" She arched her neck to indicate what she meant, her nose scrunching. "Just don't take too much."

"Yeah, that's not happening."

Her brow furrowed. "Why not?"

"Because it's not happening." And I wouldn't feed on someone else in front of her either. "Let's just watch Kols."

It appeared he was close to seducing his little brunette into a cove, where he would kiss her deeply, move to her neck, and nibble. She'd liken the whole experience to receiving a hickey—one that may or may not result in an orgasm. It depended on her intensity levels pre-bite.

"I don't want to watch Kols," Ella snapped. "I want you to bite me."

"No." *And I refuse to discuss it further.* "Focus on—" I caught her wrist as she started to walk away. "Where the hell are you going?"

She yanked out of my hold and continued moving without a word.

I glanced upward and prayed for patience before stalking after her. I found her outside of the club on the sidewalk, walking in the general direction of the portal we'd arrived through. "Isabella," I said, trying again to grab her. But she moved out of my reach and spun around to thrust her finger against my chest.

"Don't you 'Isabella' me, Trayton Nacht. If you're not going to show me what to do, then I'm just going home."

I folded my arms. "Yeah? How? You don't even know the code or how to activate the lift."

She narrowed her gaze. "You're an asshole, you know that?"

"Wow, we're back to square one already?" I feigned shock. "Here I thought it'd be at least another hour before you picked a pointless fight with me."

Her hand lifted, but I caught her wrist before her palm could connect with my face. I walked her backward into the alley, pressing her up against the wall. My powers triggered, igniting a cloak of sorts to hide our quarrel from anyone passing by. A natural response that I'd used countless times to disguise my feedings, but I had no intention of biting Ella right now.

No, I wanted to fucking throttle her.

"Were you just about to *hit* me?" I demanded.

"You're being a dick." She tried to extract herself.

I pinned her thighs with my own and caged her smaller body between my arms. "Stop, Isabella."

"You stop, Trayton," she retorted, her blue eyes glimmering with fury and restrained power as she glowered up at me. "If you want Kols to teach me about biting so bad, then I'll ask him to show me. But I want a *real* demonstration, not just to watch from the kid's corner."

"Did you just suggest you want my brother to bite you?" Flames erupted on my fingertips with the words. "Have you lost your fucking mind?"

"No, but you clearly have! What was the point of bringing me here if you weren't going to actually teach me anything?"

"I was teaching you until you stomped off like a little princess throwing a tantrum."

She gasped. "Fuck you, Tray."

Jesus! "What the hell is wrong with you? I haven't done anything wrong."

"You're being an obstinate jerk and not explaining anything to me."

"Do you even hear yourself?" I wondered out loud, flabbergasted. "I've spent the last month doing exactly the opposite."

"So why won't you bite me?" she asked, her gaze narrowing.

"Fuck," I breathed, my head falling back. "Is that what this is about? The fact that I won't bite you?"

"No," she said, the word too fast for it to be believable. "It's that you won't tell me why. You're acting all high and mighty, saying it won't happen, that I should watch Kols, and refusing to elaborate."

I softened a little at her explanation, hearing the words she refused to say that were carefully threaded between the admission.

She wanted to know why I wouldn't bite her.

Because she wanted me to bite her.

I palmed her cheek and pressed my forehead to hers.

"Ella, when a male fae bites a female fae with a compatible bloodline, it initiates a mating process. If I bite you, you'll become mine. Permanently. Because there's no going back once a male fae has initially claimed a female fae."

Her only response was a puff of air.

"It technically takes three bites," I continued softly. "The first is more the dating phase, the second is an engagement period, and the third is a mating for life. And it can only be initiated by a male fae." Which was a source of contention among the Midnight Fae.

Our females were rarely given a choice in the higher circles. Even Ella's mother, who had chosen a human, would have eventually been called back to fulfill her familial obligations.

Just as Ella would one day be forced to accept me.

That I *wanted* her to make the choice herself was merely a personal preference on my part. Not all male fae felt that way.

But Kols and I were raised a little differently. Our mother was rather keen on the *human modernist movements*, as she called them.

"Wh-what about me being a Halfling?" Ella asked softly, her blue eyes wide and holding mine. "I'm still part human."

"Your fae bloodline overrides the other." I lowered my hand from her cheek down to her hip, gently grasping her as I placed my other arm against the wall over her head.

"You're sure?"

I nodded. "I sensed it the moment we met in that alley years ago. Your royal line was like a buzzing energy that warmed my skin, marking you as a potential mate. It's why we tend to get carried away when we kiss."

Her pupils flared. "Because our blood makes us want more..." Her cheeks flushed a pretty shade. "Things."

I chuckled. "Things?"

"You know what I mean."

"Sex?" I suggested. "Intimacy?"

That only made her cheeks darken to a gorgeous red as

she bobbed her head in affirmation.

"Oh, Ella, that's not just our magical compatibility." I slid my thigh between hers, my grip tightening on her hip. "*We* want more because we're attracted to one another. Our Elite bloodlines are only a small piece of the puzzle." I knew plenty of mated pairs where one side—typically the female—despised the other.

"But our connection adds to the, uh, heat, right?" She cleared her throat. "Like, that's why I want you to bite me?"

My blood heated at her question. "You want me to bite you?"

She nodded shakily, her eyes holding mine. "I… I, yeah. I think I do."

"Do or did?" I asked, arching a brow. "Knowing it'll bind you to me, I assume you meant *did*."

Ella's tongue slid out to dampen her lips, her throat working as she fought to swallow. "Do," she whispered.

My heart actually stopped. "I don't think you understand, Ella. When I bite you, there is no going back."

"But it makes you mine, too?" she asked.

I'm already yours, I thought. Out loud, I merely confirmed with, "Yes."

"So it's a two-way commitment. Is that why you won't bite me? Because you don't want a mate? I mean, you don't want me as your mate?"

Wow, how she'd turned this conversation around.

My lips parted without sound. Because I didn't know how to answer. Never in my wildest dreams would I have anticipated having this conversation now, here, in London, outside a club. She had to be freezing, too, with the wintry temperatures settling in around us. Yet her cheeks remained a rosy red.

Because she's a fae.

I wondered if she even realized her immunity to the chill surrounding us.

No, she was too consumed by the biting inquiry.

She thought I didn't want to claim her. It was written in

the uncertainty of her expression, the way her lower lip wobbled just slightly as if she expected my rejection.

How far we'd come in a month.

Hell, how far we'd come in the last hour.

She'd just tried to hit me ten minutes ago. Now she wanted me to mark her.

"I do want a mate," I told her softly. "All fae males crave the bond, but it's often one-sided. Our society—the Council—assigns royal pairings. Kols, for example, is betrothed to Emelyn Jyn. But they hate each other."

Well, that wasn't exactly true. Emelyn absolutely wanted to fuck Kols. However, her familial line was known for using physical persuasion as a way to manipulate their mates.

Fortunately, my brother thought with his brain more than with his dick.

"Oh." Ella's nose scrunched, her body stiffening. "Wait. That means you're promised to someone already?"

"I am." I lowered my arm from the wall, my palm wrapping around the back of her neck. I could already see the anger brewing in her gaze, the assumptions being made. I killed them with a statement I knew would either destroy our tenuous connection or strengthen it.

I really hoped for the latter.

"The Council assigned me to you, Ella. *You* are my betrothed."

CHAPTER SIXTEEN

✿ ELLA ✿

YOU ARE MY BETROTHED.

Those four words reverberated in my head on repeat, my mouth opening and closing without sound.

A thrill ran down my spine, chased by a chill of reality.

"That's why you're here," I managed to say on a breath. "That's why you want to help me. The Council made you."

He snorted. "I'm here because I want to be. Unlike my brother, I was provided with options for my mating. I chose you."

I blinked. *What?* "When?"

"Six months ago."

Okay... that was, well, unexpected. "Why?" I croaked out. He didn't even know me then. Well, outside of running into me in an alley. That hardly even counted as an introduction.

"Why did I choose you?" he asked, his gaze searching mine.

Sure, we can go with that. I nodded because speaking required air, and I seemed to have forgotten how to breathe.

He released my neck to palm the back of his own, his opposite hand still on my hip. "It's complicated." I expected him to leave it at that, but he surprised me by continuing. "That night we first met, you were so utterly broken. I'd never seen anyone so shattered in my life, and the sight honestly took my breath away. Rage unlike anything I've ever felt overwhelmed me. I wanted to kill the human who put you in that powerless state.

"But I couldn't. So I followed you home to ensure you were safe. Then I gave the information to the Council. Your identity was clear to me through our instant blood connection, your royal line a famous one. My father looked over your situation personally—you saw his notes in the file."

I recalled the documents he'd given me last month and nodded. There'd been detailed reports about the death of my parents and my subsequent upbringing by Clarissa. The early notes didn't comment on my treatment, just stating I was in a home with means and would receive a proper human education.

It was the last two years of documentation that included information on Ryan, Carmen, Dash, and Charlie.

"Well, your file was given to me about half a year ago as a potential candidate. And when I saw how much you'd endured, my heart broke for you all over again. But then, I saw the fighter in the details. The way you handled every situation thrown your way with grace and determination. And I knew then that you were the one for me." He released his neck. "Fuck, I think I even knew the night we met. Your touch was magic. I'd never felt anything like it in my seventeen years. And I never forgot it."

Seventeen years? "Wait… How old are you?"

His brow furrowed. "Twenty, why?"

"I didn't realize you were older than me." Some sense settled into me with that admission. "Wait, how much do I really know about you?"

He gave me a look. "We've spent the last month together, where I've outlined every detail of fae life, including that of my history. I'd say you know quite a bit."

"But I didn't know your age or that we're apparently *betrothed* by a council of fae." I frowned. "Saying that out loud makes it sound insane."

"Because you've grown up in the human world, where mortals date for endless months or years, wed, divorce, and start all over again."

"That's a bit of a generalization. Not everyone divorces," I pointed out.

"But they do spend an awfully long time—given their short time spans—dating before marriage."

Okay, he had a point, but... "Again, not all of them."

"Regardless, what I'm trying to say is that your standards are dictated by your human experience. Fae are very different."

I twisted my lips to the side, a memory of something he'd said about my mother's marriage to my father nagging at me. "You said my dad wouldn't have been able to move on had he been a fae."

"Right. Because fae mate for life."

"Meaning, if you bite me, we're together forever."

"Yes, that's what I've been trying to explain."

"And you didn't want to bite me, even though we're betrothed according to the Council," I added, frowning. "Because you're not ready?"

"No, because I wanted you to understand the implications of my biting you. Unlike many of my kind, I don't believe in forcing a mating bond on my intended."

My eyebrows lifted. "The male fae do that?"

"All the time," he drawled, glancing over his shoulder at a group of men walking to the club.

I'd almost forgotten about our surroundings. "Did they hear us?" I wondered out loud. Except they would have stopped, right? It wasn't every day two people spoke about fae.

"No, I'm cloaking us," he replied absently. "But we should probably head back, either to Darlington or to my family condo here in the city. It's getting late."

"What about Kols?"

Tray smirked. "Oh, he'll be fine. He's either moved on to another conquest or decided that little brunette was enough for the night. Regardless, he can take care of himself."

"I thought you said he was engaged to Emma?" I asked, allowing him to pull me away from the wall and into the street.

"Emelyn," he corrected. "And yeah, he is. He also hates her with a boiling passion, so he's all about fucking around while he still can."

"Wait, if he hates her, why is he going to mate her?"

"Royal bloodlines," he replied. "Kols is the future Midnight Fae King. He's responsible for breeding the next heir, which can't be done with just anyone."

"So he has to mate a girl he hates?" That sounded ridiculous. "How archaic are your rules?"

"Compared to human society? Very." He glanced at me, something passing through his features. "My mother is very forward-thinking and trying to help change my father's mind on Kols's behalf, but so far, no luck."

He flagged down a cab, then set up some sort of muffling spell so we could continue talking freely, and dove into a discussion on the political structure of the Midnight Fae.

My primary takeaway? Males were the ruling party with no female involvement in political affairs whatsoever. And the Council, it seemed, dictated everything, particularly to the more powerful lines. It struck me as a method of control, a way to keep those with substantial gifts in proper order.

"I'm surprised there aren't protests," I said as we exited the cab. I'd been so engrossed in what Tray had to say that I wasn't even sure how long the ride took, nor did I recognize the building he led us into.

He paused at the security desk to sign something, then escorted me to an elevator that I assumed was another portal.

Except he inserted a key card from his pocket and hit the top button.

"It's a system that's been in place for hundreds of years," he finally replied, referring to my comment about protests. "Only Aswad's line has dared to question it."

"Aswad?"

"King of Death Magic," he murmured. "He's what you could call my father's direct opponent."

"Oh." I massaged my temples, as I often did when Tray spoke about the fae world and all the strange nuances.

It beat high school. That was for sure.

The elevator opened into a polished marble foyer that led to an open seating area with floor-to-ceiling windows, which overlooked what appeared to be a patio of sorts.

I blinked. "Wait. Are we still in London?" Because this place was *huge*.

He chuckled. "Yeah, dove. It's one of my family's prized locations. I figure we can stay here tonight and head back to Darlington tomorrow. Unless you think Clarissa will notice?"

"If she does, she won't care." As long as the chores were done, she couldn't care less about my activities.

I wandered down the marble stairs onto a plush white carpet and padded toward the glass, kicking my shoes off along the way. "Wow," I said, eyeing the patio beyond. I hadn't paid much attention to our adventure. "Where are we exactly?"

"Near Hyde Park."

That explained the trees in the distance. The city lights

illuminated some of the greenery, providing a calming view. "It's beautiful."

"Yes," he agreed. "My mother visits often."

"Alone?"

"My father is often tied up with Council business," he murmured, coming up behind me and handing me a glass of water.

A glance to the corner revealed a bar of sorts, which I assumed was where he magically acquired the drink. "Thanks."

He kissed my exposed shoulder. "Thank you for being here."

"Where else would I be?" I asked, then sipped the cool liquid.

"Darlington?" he suggested, lifting a brow.

I snorted. "Yeah, I'll take this any day."

"Even knowing all you do now about my world? That you have no choice in being my mate because of a council of fae who require it?"

"Or that you apparently chose me, thereby ensuring I had no choice in the matter," I added. "A fact, by the way, that you withheld from me this last month."

He had the good grace to grimace. "Yeah, that, too."

I hummed, swallowing more of the water before setting it on a glass table near the seating area. "There are worse things in life," I murmured, running my fingers along the back of the leather couch. "Losing my parents. Putting up with Clarissa, Ryan, and Carmen for five years. Dash and Charlie's games."

I supposed it all seemed rather trivial now when compared to the details Tray had disclosed. Yet somehow, all those experiences had numbed my reactions to his revelations about the fae world.

I should be running from here screaming.

Instead, I found myself turning toward the guy intended to be mine.

And not necessarily disliking what I saw.

He didn't bite me tonight because he cared about my choice. Even though I technically didn't have one, he still desired my willingness.

"What would you do if I denied our mating?" I wondered out loud.

A swirl of embers lit his dark irises. "I would work even harder to change your mind."

"And if that didn't work?"

He studied me for a long moment, then smiled. "It would. Eventually."

"How can you be so sure?" I pressed. "Maybe I'll choose to stay in my world, go to college, find a nice guy to marry, and make human babies."

His expression told me he disliked that vision, but his tone remained calm as he said, "Then I'll wait until your time with him is through and try again later in our lives."

"And do what in the interim?"

He stepped forward. "Why do you really want to have this hypothetical conversation, Ella? Just to test me? To be cruel?"

I flinched at the unveiled accusation. I hadn't meant that at all, had only—

He pinched my jaw between his thumb and finger, the grasp not necessarily painful, but not gentle either.

"What do you want me to say to you?" he continued. "What promise do you need to hear? That I'll never force myself upon you? Because I think my actions have proven that. That I'll do whatever I can to help you? To train you? To protect you? What more do you need to *know* me? Time? More kisses? Whatever it is, I'll give it to you. But I need you to tell me, Ella. Even if that means watching you marry a mortal, as you so callously suggested."

Okay, wow, I'd obviously struck a nerve.

Which, yeah. It'd been a bitchy thing to say.

In truth, I wasn't even that upset. There were worse fates than finding out I was betrothed to Trayton Nacht.

I mean, he was right. Despite our rocky beginning, he'd

proven to mostly have my best interests at heart. Heck, he'd enrolled in Darlington Academy—the epitome of hell—just to get to know me.

No, not even that.

To help me.

To protect me.

To educate me.

I couldn't deny the pull I felt toward him, the way my body seemed to cave to his every touch. There *was* a connection between us. A magical thread of electricity that hummed deep inside me each time our eyes locked, like right now.

An intensity that warmed my insides, setting off butterflies in my lower belly.

It left me feeling dizzy and intoxicated all at once, my very soul drunk on Trayton. I blamed that sensation for my irrational urges and the words inching up my throat.

What could it hurt? We were already destined to be together. Why not see what that really meant?

I had nothing to lose.

Nowhere else I'd rather be.

No other future waiting for me.

Just the Midnight Fae world. And this male who claimed to be mine.

"I know what I want from you, Tray," I said, my voice soft.

"Name it." The manner in which he responded, so quick and confident, emboldened my resolve. Because I knew he meant it. Anything I desired, he'd do it. For me. Despite the archaic tendencies dictating his kind, there was one aspect I'd finally begun to understand.

Midnight Fae took their mates—intended or otherwise—very seriously.

A lifelong bond.

A partnership engraved in blood.

A promise for eternity.

So unlike anything a human relationship could ever hope

to aspire to. And why would I want one when I could have a fae who set my blood on fire? When I could *choose* Tray?

"Bite me," I breathed, my hand wrapping around his neck. "I want you to bite me, Trayton Nacht."

Chapter Seventeen

My blood heated, the promise in her words wrapping around my rapidly beating heart. "You're sure?" I asked, my voice a rasp of sound between us.

"Yes." No hint of trepidation or uncertainty. Just pure confidence. "I want you to bite me. Now, please."

I grinned, amused. "Such a demanding little thing." Not that I was complaining. My hands circled her hips, pulling her flush against me.

"You said you're mine," she replied, her nails digging into my nape. "Now make me yours."

"Your courage floors me," I admitted, running my nose along her cheekbone. "So many would run in your position."

"I've never been normal." She arched her neck, exposing

her throat. "And I prefer it that way."

"Me, too," I agreed, my lips brushing her pulse.

Her heart rate remained miraculously steady, her breathing soft and calm, her body melting into mine.

All the signs of a willing mate.

Everything I could have possibly desired.

I shuddered against her, disbelieving of my fate for just a brief moment, wondering if I would awake and find this all to be a dream. But her sweet scent held me firmly in reality, asserting the truth of her feelings.

Mine, I thought, my tongue tracing the tender flesh of her throat.

One of my palms slid to her lower back, the other slipping upward into the tousled locks of her blonde hair. Her breath finally hitched, not with fear but with excitement, and it pushed me onward, encouraging me to strike.

I'd bitten countless humans.

Never a fae.

Prolonging the moment seemed second nature, a way to always remember my first—*my only*. Because this would be it for both of us. One mark made her mine, a link all other fae would sense.

She'd become off-limits.

As would I.

That she acquiesced so young proved her fae nature. She accepted our destiny so readily, as most Midnight Fae would in our position. The attraction between us only heightened our blood match, which was precisely the reason I originally chose her. I felt the stirrings of our compatibility when we first met, and realized why when I read her file.

This woman was my perfect mate.

And I would spend the rest of my life ensuring that she didn't regret this decision.

I kissed her neck, adoring her for allowing me to stake my claim. "Thank you," I whispered. "Thank you for trusting me."

My incisors pierced her skin before she could reply, my bite sinking into her pulse point.

She moaned my name, her arm circling my lower back as her opposite hand tightened against my neck, holding me to her. Not that I required the motivation. The first taste of her delectable essence held me captive, my mouth unable to move away, my throat already working to take as much of her into me as I possibly could.

Power swam around us.

Electricity raced up and down our limbs.

The bond was immediate, her psyche and soul joining mine in a blood promise. Possessiveness rolled over me, the need to claim every inch of her a darkness that consumed my mind.

My palm moved from her lower back to her ass, squeezing.

Her responding groan had me growling against her neck.

"More," she panted, her hand a vise around my nape. "More, Tray."

I lifted her off the ground single-handed and walked her backward to the wall. Her legs circled my waist, placing her hot center right where I wanted her.

That little dress of hers rolled up to her hips, leaving her thighs bare.

And a snap of her panties allowed me to feel the dampness pooling in that sweet spot I so desperately wanted to taste.

She didn't hold back, her moans matching the neediness of her hips as she pressed into my groin.

A Midnight Fae's bite always intensified sexual encounters, but this was more than just our initial mating. This was the fae beneath her skin coming out to claim her male, just as my inner fae demanded I take my female.

I released her neck, licking the wound closed with a hint of magic, and slanted my mouth over hers.

She kissed me as though she needed me to breathe.

And I gave her all the life she required with my tongue.

144

My blazer hit the floor, her exploring hands running all over my back and arms. I captured her face between my palms, dictating our kiss while allowing her to set the playing field for what came next.

Each writhing thrust against my aching cock sent sparks flying. Literally. Because my magic was out of control for this girl. All I wanted was to sink into her damp heat, to bathe my arousal in her own, and to give her every piece of my soul in the process.

This woman owned me.

Every lick, nip, and kiss sealing the promise between our souls.

"Take me to bed," she whispered.

A quiver worked its way up my spine, my feet already moving before my hands could grip her hips. She clung to me with her thighs, her eagerness a slick presence I longed to indulge in.

Her back hit the mattress of my bed—one I rarely used but was about to thoroughly put to the test. I climbed over her, bracing on my hands as her fingers went to the buttons of my dress shirt. They practically popped off in her hurry to get to my skin, her appreciative gaze stroking my torso and heightening my yearning with each passing second.

I helped her remove the fabric as it hit my shoulders, shrugging out of the material and smiling when she pushed me to my back with her palm on my chest. Her lips tasted my jaw, my neck, my pecs and abs. Each kiss a tantalizing caress that heated my blood even more.

I fisted my fingers in her hair as she reached my belt, her blue eyes peering up at me with questions in their depths. "You set the pace," I told her, refusing to take anything from her that she didn't readily agree to give.

She popped the buckle.

Then my button.

And slid down the zipper.

"Fuck," I breathed, every inch of me burning for her. It would be so easy to flip her, to take control, to slide from my boxers into the bare heat waiting for me between her thighs.

She licked the sensitive skin just above my pants and began tugging the fabric down. It required her to move to the side temporarily, gracing me with a view of her hiked-up dress and the sweetness beneath.

My limbs locked, my desire warring with my need to allow her these precious moments of control.

But those luscious blonde curls were calling to my tongue.

My hands.

My fingers.

My *cock*.

I bit down on a groan, my hands fisting at my sides. *She's going to be the death of me*, I decided. *I will literally die because I couldn't—*

"*Ella.*" I arched off the bed, her unexpected touch nearly undoing me.

She hadn't wasted any time, her palm falling to my dick and stroking me through the thin cotton. "You're going to need to teach me."

"You're doing just fine without instruction," I assured her, my skin tightening across my abdomen.

She continued her sensual torture—which she probably considered an exploration—and drew her nails downward and upward, memorizing my length.

I hissed when she stopped, my inclination to grab her nearly overwhelming me.

Until a brush of air hit my groin.

Her gasp caused my lips to twitch. Such a beautiful sound for my ego.

An ego I soon forgot as my boxers disappeared into the pile of clothes already on the floor. I'd kicked off my shoes earlier, leaving me in only my socks—which I quickly removed.

Typically, I preferred the female to disrobe first.

But something about the way Ella admired me now

made her approach so much better.

She bent to lick the tip of my cock, her hum of approval *killing* me. "Ella," I said, my voice strained. "Baby. If you do that—" I bit off on a curse as she took me deep into her mouth.

I grabbed the bedding, demanding my cock behave and allow her to play. But *fuck*, it was a challenge in self-control.

A month of heavy making out had primed my body in so many ways that no amount of jacking off could help temper it. Which, yeah, I did. A lot. Including this morning. All to fantasies that involved this very sensation.

My fingers ran through her hair automatically, my muscles reacting despite my mental demand to let her lead. It just went against every single instinct I owned.

Can't.

Do.

This.

Much.

Longer.

My orgasm crested far too soon, forcing me to pull her away before I did something embarrassing. Her protest died on a breath as I laid her out on the bed, my thigh between hers. "I need to taste you, Ella," I said against her lips. "*Really* taste you."

I kissed a path down her throat to her cleavage, my hand finding the zipper at her side to remove the fabric in the way of my exploration.

She didn't object, her nipples beading in anticipation as soon as I revealed them. I captured one between my teeth, nibbling and sucking and loving the way her back arched off the mattress. My name fell from her lips on a harsh sound that left me grinning against her sensitive peak.

I fixed my attention on her opposite breast, giving her what she craved with my tongue while I pushed her loosened dress to her hips. "I love when you go braless," I admitted on a whisper.

"Only with dresses." Her fingers combed through my

hair, gripping my strands tightly. "Straps can be... a problem."

"Mmm," I murmured. "A good problem." I continued my path downward, my hands guiding the fabric along her legs as I went until I had her naked before me. "Spread your thighs for me, Ella. Invite me to devour you."

Her blue eyes smoldered, a challenge in her gaze as she slowly obeyed.

It seemed the bedroom was the one place she didn't argue.

Good to know.

I didn't waste any time in introducing her properly to my tongue, her slick heat a flavor I intended to enjoy for eternity. And I showed her that with each slow, tender stroke, up and down, in and out, over and over again.

She practically vibrated beneath my mouth, her pleasure mounting and expanding to a height I knew she'd yet to experience.

All our previous sessions involved her pressing into my thigh, and a few times against my palm—over the clothes.

This was something new.

Her cries of approval telling me this would soon become a frequent activity.

"Are you going to come for me, Ella?" I asked against her sensitive bud, my fingers sliding into her tight channel to prepare her for my much larger entry.

"Tray..." She swallowed, her head tossed back in a sexy manner that invited me to bite her all over again. "Please, Tray."

"Oh, I do enjoy hearing you beg," I mused, licking her again. "I think we'll play more with that later." But for now, I gave her what she needed, wrapping my mouth around the sensual point I knew would push her over the edge.

She fell apart on a scream that put all my fantasies to shame.

Because Ella in the throes of passion was the most beautiful sight I'd ever seen.

She didn't hold back.

Didn't shy away from her pleasure.

No, she owned every damn second.

"Wow," she breathed, coming back down, her hair fanned around her in an illustrious wave that beckoned to my fingers.

I crawled over her, kissing her soundly and allowing her to taste herself on my tongue.

She whimpered in response, a needy little sound that had my cock throbbing against her wetness below.

"Are you okay with this?" I asked her softly, my palms cradling her face while I held her gaze. "We can stop right now, Ella. It's your decision."

She shivered, her pupils dilating.

And then she wrapped her legs around my waist, placing me directly at her entrance.

"Be gentle with me," she whispered.

"I'll always be whatever you need," I vowed, taking her mouth to seal my pledge to her.

She moaned as I slid inside her, slowly expanding her inch by inch, and flinched when I hit the barrier marking her as untouched. I pushed through, knowing it would hurt and silently promising to make it better for her as soon as she finished adjusting.

Her nails bit into my back.

Her breath hitched.

Her body locked around me.

I paused, lifting my head to watch her expression, noting the beautiful agony and pleasure mixing in her features.

When she swallowed and nodded, I continued, paying careful attention to her changing emotions.

Concern.

Acceptance.

Confusion.

Pleasure.

Her lips parted, a soft gasp escaping her as I slid out and back in, allowing her to feel the fullness of my entry.

Introducing her to a tender pace. Making love to her. Worshiping her. Claiming her. Allowing her to own me in return.

It went on for minutes, maybe hours.

Until finally she urged me to *really* move, her arousal mounting between us with each stroke. I felt it in the way she clamped down around me, her cravings lashing out at me through the scoring of her fingertips.

I introduced her to our bond.

Our mating.

Our future.

Driving her to the precipice of oblivion and sinking my teeth into her flesh to hold her there while I followed her to the edge.

And tumbled into a world of dark ecstasy with her, our bond skyrocketing to another level as a result of my second bite.

The source of our power reverberated its approval, swathing us in a sea of vitality and strength. Joining our spirits, our futures, and our hearts in a bond of eternity neither of us could ever break.

Cemented together.

Two hearts beating as one.

Mates.

CHAPTER EIGHTEEN

❧ ELLA ❧

MY BODY TINGLED ALL OVER from Tray's attentions.

He'd made love to me several times throughout the night, and again this morning in the shower before begrudgingly returning me to Darlington.

I couldn't stop smiling, even through my chores. Which were substantial today, thanks to the snow that fell overnight.

Shovel this, Ella.

Shovel that, Ella.

I chanted the words in my head, grinning the entire time. Because I finally felt alive. Like for the first time in my life, I belonged somewhere.

By Tray's side.

It was hard to part ways this morning, but we still had a

plan to carry out. However, I wanted to up our timeline. What was the point of graduating high school if I had to attend the Midnight Fae Academy next year?

A human degree wouldn't be worth much in Tray's world. His kind were essentially homeschooled until a certain age, the parents or tutors within their communities providing their general education and magical instruction. Then they attended the Academy, where they all mastered their powers and decided their place within their designated sects.

I would join the royal community, not just because of my mating to Tray, but because of my bloodline. That was where Elite—

Something hit my back, shoving me forward. My knees hit the pavement, the thin fabric of my jeans ripping on impact. I just barely saved my face by catching myself on my palms. "*Shit,*" I hissed as a tinkle of laughter sounded overhead.

Ryan.

"Careful, Cindersoot," she drawled. "Daydreaming can be dangerous."

Carmen's booted foot appeared by my head. "I bet she's thinking about wherever she disappeared to last night."

"Yes, where were you all night, Ella?" Ryan asked, coming to stand beside her twin.

Scowling, I shoved off the ground, only to be kicked hard in the abdomen. I curled onto my side, protecting my now tender torso.

"Sorry, slipped," Ryan said.

I snorted. "Right." Now my body tingled for an entirely new reason—*rage.*

"Well, where were you?" Carmen demanded.

"None of your fucking business," I retorted, scowling up at her.

Both of her sculpted eyebrows shot upward. "*Excuse me?*"

"Sorry, for the hard of hearing, that means *fuck you.*" I

rolled away before Ryan's foot could "slip" again and scrambled backward in the snowy yard.

"Did she really just say that to me?" Carmen asked. Her shock would have been comical if Ryan wasn't already stalking after me.

I was so not in the mood for this game today.

With a strength fueled by adrenaline, I came up to my feet and held up my hands in front of me. "Try it," I dared her.

Ryan threw back her head and laughed, the sound holding a touch of crazed cruelty. "Wow. Now I really want to know where you were last night. Something, or maybe *someone*, has really lit a fire under your ass."

Carmen trekked into the yard, grimacing as the wintry mix touched her jeans.

She'd likely throw them away tonight, claiming they were too soiled to wear again.

Spoiled bitch.

"Where were you?" she repeated, clearly not getting the message the first time.

So I tried a different approach. "In England." I mean, that was the truth. She just wouldn't believe me.

"Cute," she snapped. "Tell us where you were, or we'll tell Mom you snuck out for the night."

I shrugged. "Go for it." What the hell could Clarissa do to me? I was eighteen and no longer needed her expensive education.

Ryan reached for me and I grabbed her wrist.

A shock of energy traveled between us, sending her several feet backward with a curse as she collapsed into the snow.

Oh, shit...

"What the hell was that?" Carmen shrieked, looking between me and Ryan.

"The bitch just shocked me!" her sister cried, cradling her wrist.

I rolled my eyes and said the first thing that came to my

mind. "Sorry. I slipped."

Carmen spun around, pinning me with a harsh look, and made the mistake of trying to poke me in the chest.

That mere touch put her on her ass, energy humming protectively around me.

Is Tray doing this somehow? I wondered.

"Mother!" Ryan shouted, drawing my attention back to the wicked stepsisters on the ground.

Carmen was out cold.

Huh. That's new.

I lifted my hands to examine them while Ryan continued to call for Clarissa. I ignored her, too busy gaping at the blue embers dancing between my fingertips.

Holy crap...

I barely registered Clarissa's angry voice, the sound at my back as I began walking away from the house. They could finish shoveling, for all I cared. This was far more important.

Because either my powers had just flared to life or Tray had put a protective spell around me.

In any case, I had questions only my mate could answer.

Fortunately, I knew where to find him.

Unfortunately, it was a several-mile walk.

With a groan, I turned back around to find my bike, only to be stopped by a very angry stepmother in the driveway. "Where do you think you're going, young lady?"

"Out," I replied, pushing past her and smiling at her shocked gasp behind me.

Another idea occurred to me, one that had my lips pulling upward as I headed into the garage.

Why bother with the bike?

I'd take a car instead.

Finding Ryan's keys on the wall, I twirled them around my finger and approached her prized possession. She bellowed from the yard, coming to her feet. But I already had the door closed and locked before she hit the semi-shoveled pavement.

This would be a fun experience.

I knew how to drive because Clarissa taught me—how else would I get groceries for the family on Sundays?

But I'd never taken Ryan's pretty baby for a spin.

Her sporty little two-seater purred to life, drowning out the shouts of my monsterous stepfamily.

Ryan had the brilliant idea to jump into the middle of the driveway as I hit reverse.

I focused on her in the mirror and backed out of the garage, deciding a game of chicken could be fun. I almost hoped she called my bluff.

But as expected, she jumped out of the way at the last moment, her curses lost to the rev of the engine.

I gave them all a little wave, grinning at their flabbergasted expressions, and gunned it out of the neighborhood.

Oh, there would be hell to pay later.

So worth it, I thought, navigating the freshly plowed roads with ease.

Tray stood waiting for me on his porch, a broad smile on his face as I parked Ryan's car haphazardly in the street. Maybe I'd get lucky and someone would scrape along the side of it.

"I sensed your magic," he said as he sauntered toward me. "What'd you do? Other than steal the queen bitch's car?"

"I zapped her," I said, holding up my hands to show him the still-flickering embers. "Is it a protection spell or something?"

He took my wrist to examine the blue sparks. "A protection spell?"

"Like something you did?"

His amused eyes lifted to mine. "No, El. This is all you, baby." He laced our fingers together, the hum of electricity sizzling between us and intensifying. "Your power is growing by the second." He sounded excited, tugging me through the threshold into his house and closing the door with his foot.

"It wasn't doing that until you touched me," I whispered, marveling at the current heightening between us. "All I did was grab Ryan's wrist, and it jolted her. Then Carmen tried to poke me, and the same thing happened, only it knocked her out."

"Your inner fae is coming alive," he said, leading me into the kitchen. "What did they do?"

"Shoved me," I muttered. "Kicked me, too."

His nostrils flared, his grip tightening. "That explains the spell you evoked. It's instinctual barrier magic. Or protection, as you surmised."

"But you didn't cast it?"

He shook his head. "No, *you* did."

"How?"

"Natural defense. Similar to the fight-or-flight response. Your fae chose to fight." He cracked another smile. "Ryan and Carmen are lucky to be alive."

I told him how I almost hit Ryan with her own car.

Which earned me a harsh laugh in response.

"Too bad," he drawled. "Wouldn't have killed her, but I'd enjoy seeing that bitch in a wheelchair."

As cruel as it sounded, I couldn't exactly disagree. "We need to take them down, Tray." Because once I was gone, they'd just find a replacement target. "I can't let them pull this shit with someone else. The same goes for Dash and Charlie."

He palmed my cheek, his skin sizzling against mine. "We'll destroy them," he vowed, brushing his mouth over mine. "But first, we need to tame your power. Before you burn my house down."

I frowned. Yeah, I felt hot, but not *that* hot. "I'm hardly about to explode."

"No?" He cocked a brow and glanced over my shoulder. "Then why is my dining room on fire?"

I spun around and gasped at the sapphire flames dancing over the wood table.

And crawling up the wall.

"Oh…" I covered my mouth.

He circled my waist with his arms, his head touching mine as the fire slowly died, leaving scorch marks behind. "I need you to close your eyes, Isabella."

"Because that'll help?" I scoffed, cringing as another inferno spun to life a few feet away.

"Shh, trust me," he whispered. "Close your eyes and picture yourself in the water, listening to the waves rushing the shore. Each cool, crisp drop touching the sand and drawing back, to rush forward again. Rhythmic. Soothing. Serene."

My breath raced out of me, his words seeming to calm some chaotic nerve inside me. I clutched his hands, holding on as I allowed the vision into my mind.

"It's flowing around you," he continued softly. "All the water in the world, rippling beneath your fingertips, caressing your skin, blessing your spirit. Allow it to kiss you, Ella. Allow it to consume you."

I shuddered, my vision morphing into a whirlpool, swirling me in a violent circle, drawing me deeper into a black hole of madness and away from the sunlight.

"Don't fight it." Tray's lips were at my ear. "It's not nearly as dark as it appears. I'm waiting for you there. Seek out our connection. Find me."

Inky ropes ensnared my waist, pulling me deeper. I whimpered, my heart jumping in my chest.

This couldn't be right.

But I couldn't open my mouth to speak, the very real snakelike bands encircling my head and covering my lips.

Yanking me under.

Into a sea of perpetual *magic*.

I blinked into my new oblivion, sparkling strands dancing beneath the surface and twining in glittering bands.

One blinked brighter than the others, a beckoning of sorts, waving in the thick, dark waters.

I swam toward it, my body suddenly free of the binds.

Each stroke stirred a sense of rightness in my gut.

Each kick awakened a new purpose.

Until I reached the light and realized it wasn't a light at all, but Tray.

He welcomed me with open arms, his body a familiar warmth against mine, and spun me in a circle, his pride a kiss against my very spirit.

I opened my eyes to find him gazing down at me with unshed tears in his eyes. "You're beautiful, Ella," he marveled, his expression radiating an emotion that warmed my heart. "The most beautiful Midnight Fae I've ever seen."

His mouth captured mine, his kiss igniting a tornado of sensations inside me.

Heat engulfed me from head to toe.

I threw my arms around his neck, no longer caring about the importance of breathing. He lifted me onto the counter, stepping in between my thighs and dominating me with his tongue.

Somehow our clothes disappeared.

Maybe I burned them off.

Maybe he used magic.

All I cared about was our joining below, which happened so suddenly and yet not fast enough. Tray drove into me, his lips catching my shocked cry, and his hands branding my sides.

It felt so ethereal, as if we were making love in a dream and not in his kitchen.

My body vibrated with *need*.

Words fell from my mouth like a chant.

He whispered my name in worship against my ear, my neck, my breasts.

Every touch resembled a claim, every kiss a promise, every thrust an introduction to the future.

I was utterly owned by Trayton Nacht.

My head fell back on a scream, his teeth sinking into my neck.

Smoky ribbons circled us, the ethereal energy a seal I felt

to my very soul. My heart accepted the intrusion, allowing an anchor to settle against my chest—one I felt tied to Tray.

Mine, Tray whispered into my thoughts, sending a shiver down my spine. *You're mine, Ella. Just as I'm yours.*

And he proved it by opening his mind to me.

Every emotion. Every feeling. Every thought. Suddenly mingled with mine.

It shot my ecstasy to a whole new level as he increased his pace, his thrusts turning sharper and harder with each passing second. I'd already reached oblivion once, and he wanted to take me there again—this time with him along for the ride.

His mounting need provoked mine, forcing me to new heights as he took us both over the edge on a groan I felt all the way to my toes.

This was how fae mated.

Underlined in magical currents.

Stirring fire into the air.

And leaving both participants replete in the best way.

My forehead fell to his shoulder, my mind thoroughly blown.

Do I really have to go to school tomorrow? I wondered, preferring this to classes.

Tray chuckled, his lips a caress against my hair. *Mmm, I think we can find ways to make it interesting.*

I started, his voice warm and *real* in my mind.

Our new connection hadn't truly registered before, but I understood it now. *You're in my head.*

As you're in mine, he replied, drawing back to cup my cheek. "I've bitten you three times in the last twenty-four hours."

"So our mating is, uh, complete?"

He nodded, his eyes closely studying mine.

I stared right back at him.

And he smiled. "You don't regret it."

"Why would I?" I'd told him last night to bite me. I knew what it meant. I accepted it then, just as I did now.

"Because we belong to each other for eternity, Ella."

"Yeah, well, you're the one who should be scared off by that, Nacht," I informed him. "Not me."

"How do you figure that?"

"Because now you're stuck with me," I replied, grinning evilly. "And apparently, I like to set things on fire."

Such as the kitchen island behind him.

He smothered it without looking, his power a wave of energy that I *felt* caress mine. *How interesting,* I mused, enjoying the sensation that awoke.

"Good thing I like it hot," Tray murmured against my lips, smiling. "And there's no one else I'd rather be glued to, Ella."

My mouth was suddenly too occupied to voice a reply.

Which was fine by me.

I let my mind and heart do the talking for me.

And allowed him to take me to new heights, over and over again.

CHAPTER NINETEEN

TRAY

I DUMPED A BAG OF O NEGATIVE into the blender, eliciting a grimace from Ella. She sat on the island counter in my shirt, her exposed legs a sexy reminder of the lack of clothes beneath the fabric.

"Are you really making a milkshake with blood in it?" she asked, her nose scrunching upward as I added a scoop of vanilla ice cream to the mix.

"Yup." I had meant to feed last night but instead bit my mate. While I didn't regret it, I felt the repercussions of tapping into the source of our magic without the requisite fuel.

"That's disgusting," she said.

I smirked. "We'll see how you feel after you've tasted it."

"I am not drinking that."

"You're going to try it," I countered, hitting the button before she could argue. As soon as it finished, I started speaking again to thwart her attempts at an argument. "When Midnight Fae are young, we can't exactly venture into the Human Realm for sustenance. Most don't start until they're thirteen or fourteen. So we've developed other creative ways to imbibe the essence without having to bite."

Her expression said I hadn't changed her mind.

"Consider it an energy drink," I added. "We just expelled a lot of power, Ella. You might not feel it yet, but you will. Unless you accept my offering."

"I've never had to drink blood before."

"You've also never danced with your fae gifts before." I poured the contents into two glasses and plucked a pair of straws from the drawer. "Trust me, dove. You need this. As do I."

My limbs were beginning to shake, the first sign of exhaustion setting in. I'd be hurting by morning. The only reason I'd gotten away without feeding since arriving was because I hadn't tapped into my abilities as often as usual.

And, uh, yeah, the last few hours with Ella had more than made up for my lack of use.

I took a sip of the liquid, testing it before sliding the opposite glass across the island to Ella.

"What does it taste like?" she asked, her nose still doing that adorable scrunching thing.

"Try it and find out," I dared. It wouldn't taste at all like she was expecting. Humans typically described the flavor as salty or coppery. That wasn't what Midnight Fae experienced. For example, her blood was ambrosia to my tongue—sweet and addicting. My drink was dull in comparison, but it satisfied my hunger. I took several more sips while watching her, challenging her with my eyes.

Unless you're scared, I said into her mind.

That taunt received the desired effect and had her grabbing the drink. "When I puke, I'll be sure to aim in your direction."

My lips twitched. "Okay, darling." I took another healthy swallow as she positioned the straw between her lips.

Her eyes closed, her face grimacing as she hollowed her cheeks.

And then her forehead creased.

She took another deep pull, her eyes reopening in surprise. "Why is this so good?"

"Because you're a Midnight Fae," I replied with a wink.

We fell into a comfortable silence while we both finished our energizing snack. She licked the rim when she finished all the liquid. I pretended not to see it, not wanting to tease her and spoil the moment.

I cleaned up the kitchen, then leaned back against the sink and folded my arms. Her gaze went to my boxers and down to my exposed thighs before slowly traveling up my naked torso to my face.

Amusement warmed my chest. "Mmm, I adore that invitation in your eyes, Ella."

"Then why are you standing over there?" she asked, her brow inching upward. "To tease me?"

"No, to keep from touching you." We needed to let the blood work its way through our system before we played again. Another trip to the dark source would lay me out on my ass right now, and I'd prefer to avoid the embarrassment. "We should talk about our next steps."

She frowned. "What do you mean? I thought we were mated already."

"Oh, we are," I assured her, smiling at the relief in her features. "We belong to each other completely. I was talking about the evil bitchlets and their merry gang of idiots."

Ella snorted a laugh. "Merry gang of idiots."

"If the shoe fits," I drawled, splaying my hands out before me in an innocent gesture.

"Oh, it fits," she agreed. "As for next steps, I think I just initiated phase one today."

"I think you did, too." Which was why I wanted to discuss our plan of action.

"I don't want to go back there, Tray."

"Then don't." I waved to the hallway that led to two living rooms and the grand staircase. "I have plenty of space here. And you're welcome in my bed anytime."

Her lips twisted to the side and she sighed. "Then Clarissa will stop paying for my tuition."

"Also not an issue. I'll just pick up the payments." I shrugged. "What's mine is yours now anyway. Isn't that the human saying?"

She wasn't thrilled by the idea. "You're not paying my tuition to Darlington Academy."

"I'd rather do that than have you suffer in that house anymore. Besides, we can use it to our advantage. If Ryan asks, I can tell her I promised to pay your winter semester tuition, something I'll say is all part of my master plan— playing the part of savior in your life to win you over. It'll add to the bomb I'm supposed to drop on you when I tell you it was all a game. I'll just say I plan to remove your tuition as well, leaving you homeless and without a school to attend. She'll love it."

My heart hurt just thinking about the idea, but I soothed myself in knowing it would never happen.

Ella was mine.

I would protect her until my dying breath.

"You're right. She'll love that." Ella sounded rather irritated by the prospect, a dark gleam entering her gaze. "Teaching her a lesson isn't going to be enough, is it?"

"Given her penchant for tormenting you, no, I don't think it is."

"We need to take them all down first—except her. It'll isolate her so when we impose the grand finale, she'll have nowhere to run and no one to lean on for help. Make her feel as alone and helpless as she's made me all these years."

I nodded, liking this direction. "Keep going."

"Let's add Clarissa to the list. Hell, let's add the entire damn academy. They've all sat back and watched me suffer without doing a thing to help me. Clarissa has gone as far as to applaud and encourage the behavior." Ella hopped off the counter to begin pacing, ideas churning in her mind and leaving her mouth at the same time. I observed while she worked, only adding my opinion when asked, and by the end, we had a solid plan of action.

"Tomorrow we start by taking the school," she said, finishing our discussion, excitement pouring off her in waves. "And I know just how we'll kick-start the takedown."

CHAPTER TWENTY

TRAY

ELLA'S PLAN TO SHOW UP at the academy the
following morning in Ryan's car was brilliant.

Everyone stood gaping.

And not just because of the brand-new fitted uniform
Ella sported as we walked hand in hand toward the entrance.

It was her entire attitude that captured their attention.
And obviously Ryan's sporty little car with the jagged
scratch down the side.

Ella's bracelet touched my wrist, sending a zap up my
arm. I'd gifted her the silver cuff this morning, the magic-
laced metal meant to help temper her abilities. Just so she
didn't accidentally burn the school down.

Not that I'd begrudge her for such an act.

This place deserved to melt into a pile of ash.

As well as the majority of the humans inside it.

But I wanted to give Ella time to foster her talents and learn how to control them, and the beauty on her wrist would help.

The twin bitchlets stood waiting at the front doors, their fuming expressions highly amusing.

An amusement Ella only heightened when she casually tossed Ryan the car keys. "Thanks for the ride, sis."

I draped my arm over her shoulders and kissed her cheek. "Thank *you* for the ride," I whispered in her ear, eliciting a giggle from my mate. She knew exactly what I meant.

"You're so dead," Ryan warned, steam practically billowing from her ears.

Ella and I ignored her, my shoulder bumping Carmen's as we pushed through the doorway and into the school.

Several students gawked at the showdown, their shock palpable.

Sheep, Ella thought at them, her mental tone one of annoyance.

They just need a new leader, I told her.

That's not going to be me.

No, I imagine you have no desire to manage these fools. They'd all stood by for years and observed her humiliation. She owed them nothing.

We stopped at our lockers to pick up our books and made our way to the English classroom while everyone watched.

They really were pathetic humans. Even the so-called adults of the academy were pitiful. No backbones, all driven by class and greed.

I sat beside Ella rather than in front of her, my arm sprawled across the back of her chair. After a long conversation last night, we decided to bump up our timeline. There was something bitterly poetic about our new and improved plan. It would require me to say a few things I'd hate, but our blossoming link would keep our minds open and honest.

You could profess undying love to Ryan, and I'd know you're full of shit, Ella murmured, having heard my thoughts.

I snorted. *You wouldn't need to be able to read my mind to know that.*

Her lips quirked up. *True.*

Charlie sauntered into the room, his steps faltering as he caught sight of me beside Ella. My lips curled. *Oh, look, Ella sweetheart. Phase two is about to begin.*

No. It already started. Her gaze positively glittered. *Ready to have some fun?*

I thought you'd never ask. And as this part of the plan was my suggestion, I couldn't wait to watch the fireworks.

It'd take a few weeks, but I already set some of the pieces in motion this morning.

Now we just had to wait.

And, in the interim, begin our task of taking over the school.

We'd give them all a king and queen to adore, then shatter all their hearts at once.

* * *

ELLA SAT IN THE MIDDLE OF THE CAFETERIA, resembling a queen. My lips curled at the sight, adrenaline thrumming through my veins.

It'd been two weeks since our notorious arrival on campus in Ryan's car, and everything had changed since.

She now lived with me and spent every night in *our* bed.

Several students were flocking toward her, seeking shelter beneath her growing wings. Something Ella only allowed because the majority of them had endured bullying, just not on the same scale as her.

It helped that Ryan and Carmen were allowing it, mostly because they thought this would only add to their stepsister's eventual fall. What they failed to realize was that we were slowly swaying the kingdom in Ella's favor.

Dash seemed to be the only one not keen on this plan.

Charlie, being a perpetual dumbass, thought it was great. I suspected he hoped to be the one to lick Ella's wounds— whether he had her cooperation or not.

Which was why I couldn't wait for today's events to unfold.

We'd decided to take him down first.

By dismantling his status.

I leaned against the wall and checked my watch. It should be any moment now that he received a phone call. One that would destroy his world.

Where's my kiss? Ella asked, her eyes glittering from across the room.

I smirked at her. *Such a demanding little mate you are.*

Damn straight.

I started toward her, ready to oblige, when Ryan caught my arm and tugged me backward. My gaze locked on hers, my eyebrow inching upward. "Yes?"

"Meet me in the hallway in five minutes."

"Why?"

She gave me a seductive look that rotted my insides. "I want to reward you for all your hard work."

I forced my lips to curl despite my urge to vomit.

In no way did I ever want a *reward* from this vile creature.

"As tempting as that is, this plan hinges on my ability to win over my conquest. Which isn't going to happen if she finds out I'm playing on the side." I carefully removed her hand from my bicep, making a show of my rejection for those observing.

Our voices were pitched too low for anyone to overhear, but body language could be a telling indicator of a conversation.

Something I played upon by folding my arms and taking on a condemning stance.

"I'm very close, Ryan," I said softly. "Unless you've decided to skip the fireworks and go straight to my reward?"

She glanced at Ella, her expression souring. "Oh, no. I

want to see her face crumble when you tell her this was all a ruse."

"You really do hate her," I mused, cocking my head. "But I still haven't figured out why." Not exactly true. I suspected jealousy played a large factor in her treatment of her stepsister. Ella embodied beauty in a way Ryan never would. And not just because this bitch possessed a black heart.

She flipped her brown hair over her shoulder and shrugged. "She's an easy target."

"Is she?" I wondered out loud, shifting my focus to the female in question. "She's been one of my biggest challenges to date." And I meant that.

I also heard that, Ella replied into my mind.

I smothered a grin with my hand and arched a brow at Ryan. "Are we—"

"Oh my god!" Carmen jumped in between us, her back to me. "You need to see this."

"I'm in the middle of a conversation," Ryan snapped, gesturing at me over her twin's shoulder.

Carmen grabbed Ryan's hand, tugging her away while saying, "He can wait."

"I won't be waiting," I called after them, deciding we needed a crueler fate for Carmen. Ella and I had discussed something slightly more temporary for her, mostly because Ryan was the bigger culprit. Ella thought Carmen might be a different person without the influence of her twin, but I disagreed.

Both of those females deserved a lifetime of purgatory for their treatment of others.

I took two more steps, when a chorus of gasps went up around me.

Ah... It's time, I thought. That was what had Carmen's attention. Of course.

Ella stood to greet me as I made my way toward her, both of us ignoring the rising chatter throughout the room. Because we already knew.

Her gaze glittered with excitement. *I think phase two is going to be a resounding success.*

I brushed my mouth over hers, grinning. *Me, too.*

Charlie's name echoed throughout the room, and the male in question stood frozen beside a gaping Dash.

Somewhere, the news played loudly from someone's phone, announcing Anderson Motors' recent legal troubles and impending financial doom.

"Those automotive companies really should focus on safety," I put in conversationally.

Ella bit her lip to keep from giggling, her approval warming our bond.

It wasn't like I deliberately sabotaged Anderson Motors. They already had the problems. I just made them a little easier for the appropriate authorities to find.

And they acted swiftly and efficiently.

Whispers flooded the room as Charlie made his way through it—alone. Dash watched him, his expression torn between loyalty to his friend and loyalty to himself.

In the end, he chose himself.

As I suspected he would.

Anderson Motors wouldn't be recovering anytime soon, if ever. Meaning Charlie was about to go through a very humbling experience, one that would probably take him out of school or relocate him to somewhere more financially suitable.

Or maybe they'd allow him to stay to finish the year. I really hoped so because his life at Darlington Academy—a place that notably cared more about status than its students—was about to change drastically.

As Dash demonstrated now by returning to his table instead of chasing after his supposed friend.

One down, three to go, Ella murmured.

I kissed her temple and wrapped my arms around her. *On to the next phase,* I agreed.

CHAPTER TWENTY-ONE

ELLA

THREE WEEKS LATER and everyone was still talking about Charlie. He'd transferred out of Darlington Academy within days of the announcement, his family moving to somewhere in the Midwest while his father's company went to battle with an army of lawyers.

It was possible Charlie Anderson wouldn't learn anything from the experience. Perhaps I should have chosen a harsher avenue of punishment, but he was never my biggest target.

No, Dash Charming won that prize between the two of them.

He stood on the pool deck in a tiny Speedo, flirting with a trio of chicks. They were mooning over him, as per usual after swim class. He'd gotten over the disappearance of his buddy right quick, happily taking over the mantle of king at Darlington Academy.

Except something about him felt different.

Like the way his smile didn't reach his eyes. He also no longer seemed to be fucking his way through the student population. Or maybe he was just being more discreet about it. And he hadn't spent much time around Ryan or Carmen lately, at least from what I'd seen.

Regardless, he wasn't acting like the Dash I knew and loathed, and that perplexed me a bit.

With a shake of my head, I wandered into the girls' locker room, deciding to contemplate him more later.

He was next on my list after I finished fucking with Carmen.

Tray had suggested I use her as target practice for my magic. A "two birds with one stone" sort of deal whereby I familiarized myself with some of the Midnight Fae texts and spells, then applied them to my wicked stepsister.

Such as the one I evoked two days ago that induced hair loss.

It'd been a tricky spell that required a strand from her platinum blonde head, but I'd managed to snag it during lunch after pretending to bump into her.

I had used that moment to also sprinkle some dust onto her skin.

Hence the hives she'd broken out in recently—an intense case that would cause scarring if she didn't stop scratching herself.

Her appearance was the subject of conversation by all the girls in the locker room. Some felt bad for her. Others claimed karma. Most were just happy to watch her suffer.

"She's gained a ton of water weight, too," one of them was saying.

"Stress."

"Oh, totally. I mean, if my face looked like that, I'd be stress eating, too."

"Totally deserves it."

"Wish it happened to her bitch of a twin."

"Gretchen," the girl beside me warned.

"What? Ryan's a cunt. I'd love to see her suffer."

Several rounds of agreement rang through the locker area. No one would have dared hold a conversation like this a month ago. But today? Several were participating.

Down crumbles the queen, I thought, pulling my shirt over my head.

The discussion continued while I put on my skirt, socks, and shoes. It was as I put up my hair that I realized the room had fallen silent with several sets of eyes on me.

I checked my appearance, noting everything was in place.

"What?" I demanded, glaring at them all.

"Didn't you, uh, hear the announcement?" a petite junior asked. Her name began with a *T*. Taylor. Tiffany. Tia. Tribeca. Something.

"No." I had tuned out their conversation. I mean, yeah, it entertained me, but I also just wanted to get the hell out of here. "What about it?"

"You've been nominated for Winter Queen," Junior with a *T* whispered, her eyes rounding. "A-against Carmen and Ryan."

I swallowed. Well, that hadn't been part of the plan.

"Tray and Dash are up for Winter King," she continued, her voice growing a little stronger. She listed the other nominations—two senior chicks who functioned as Ryan's personal minions, and three other dudes I knew from my classes.

The typical court.

Minus me and Tray.

Did you do this? I asked him, sensing his presence in the hallway, waiting for me.

If by this, *you mean the Winter Court assignment, no.*

"Huh," I said out loud. "Cool."

Not the word I meant to use, but everyone was gaping at me.

I shrugged on my backpack and headed toward the doors. "Thanks?" I called back over my shoulder, uncertain of what else to say. The school had voted on the nominations—which meant my peers had put me into this position. Something I wasn't sure how to feel about.

"Do you think Ryan did it?" I asked as soon as I saw Tray.

He wrapped his arm around me, pulling me into his side. "It's possible, but your popularity has skyrocketed, dove. So it might be the students. We'll know when we see her reaction."

We had early release today, making swim class our last period of the day. That explained why they did the school announcements in the morning. I always tuned them out and hadn't even noticed.

Tray led me down the corridor toward the exit. Several sheep watched along the way, their intrigue palpable. *Ryan must be waiting near the doors.*

So it would seem, he murmured, tightening his hold around me as we approached her.

One look at my stepsister's face confirmed she had nothing to do with the nomination. Because she was not that good an actress.

"A word, please?" The demand was leveled at Tray, not me.

"I can't imagine what we have to discuss," he replied coolly. "I've already turned you down several times, and my decision hasn't changed."

Steam billowed from her ears as she followed us outside. "*Now,* Trayton."

"Does that actually work on other people?" He glanced at me, arching a brow. "Do you find that as annoying as I do? That people buy into this shit?"

"What can I say?" I lifted a shoulder. "I mean, she's an entitled bitch."

Ryan sputtered, my words hitting their mark and sticking.

Meanwhile, Tray nodded sagely. "It's true."

"We could just ignore her," I suggested.

He flashed me a dazzling grin. "I knew I adored you, El."

We took two steps before she shrieked, officially losing her shit. She grabbed Trayton by his blazer and yanked him backward.

My power flickered to life, zapping her on instinct.

I'd left my power-diminishing bracelet in my bag.

Oops.

She released him on a scream, her face contorting in a rage unlike any I'd ever seen. "*You!*" she yelled, pointing at me. "How are you doing that?"

I lifted my eyebrows innocently. "Doing what?"

"You know what," she snarled, stalking toward me.

But Tray stepped in between us. "I think you need to calm down, Ryan."

"That bitch electrocuted me!"

Several gasps came from our audience, their whispers becoming background noise.

"I didn't even touch you," I pointed out, pressing my palm to Tray's back. "Come on, baby. We should go."

"Oh, this is fucking rich," Ryan snapped. "He doesn't even—"

A bellow from the doorway cut her off as Carmen appeared with a giant lock of her hair in her hand.

Drawing more shocked sounds from the crowd.

Because yeah, she looked, uh, *bad.* And the words spilling from her mouth were unintelligible.

Tray's amusement touched our mating bond. *Nice.*

I try, I replied.

Carmen collapsed against Ryan—who shoved her away with a disgusted grunt. "Gross! What if you're contagious?"

Oh, I like that idea, Tray thought at me. *Can we make her contagious, dove?*

No, I need Ryan to suffer in other ways.

Disappointing. But I can wait for the finale, he replied, draping

176

his arm around me again and steering me away from the meltdown on the stairs. Everyone parted the way for us, their attention drifting between us and my evil stepsisters.

Have you given more thought about Dash? Tray asked on the way to his car.

Yeah. I think we need to take him down with Ryan. Which was what Tray had suggested. It made sense with the two of them attending the Winter Ball together.

Part of me wanted to destroy his societal status the way we'd done Charlie's, but it would be too obvious.

And to give him the same makeover as Carmen wouldn't work either.

So I decided a public humiliation for both Dash and Ryan was in order.

"Did you order the cameras?" I asked Tray after sliding into the car.

He buckled his seat belt and grinned. "Of course I did."

"Because you knew I'd cave."

"I hoped you would," he admitted, putting the car in drive. "It's also a solid way to destroy him."

"Assuming your suspicions are right," I reminded him.

"They are."

"So confident."

"Always with you." He winked at me and pulled out of the school parking lot. "But it means you need to initiate the final phase. Can you do it?"

I sighed, allowing my head to fall back on the seat. "Yeah. I can. However, I'm not going to enjoy it."

He snorted. "I should hope not."

"Aww, are you going to be jealous, Trayton Nacht?"

His palm landed on my thigh and squeezed. "You're mine, Ella. And I'm a Midnight Fae. We're notoriously possessive."

"Really? Because I don't feel that way at all," I lied, grinning at his scowl. "I have no idea why I shocked Ryan. It's not like she touched you or anything."

His scowl morphed into a chuckle. "You're a bad girl,

Isabella Cinder."

"Are you going to pun…?" I trailed off, grimacing. "Nope. Can't even say it. Too cheesy." And the words tasted horrible in my mouth.

He laughed outright, shaking his head. "Don't worry, dove. I'm not into the punishment game."

"I mean, don't get me wrong, I'd probably be fine with it. But the words? Out loud? Sounds like a cheesy romance movie."

"Pretty sure you mean porn, darling."

My eyes widened. "Fae watch porn?"

He gifted me with another of those amused sounds, the kind that made my heart skip a beat. "Oh, Ella. We're supernatural beings who thrive on blood and sex. What do you think?"

"I think I want you to share your stash."

He glanced sideways at me, then refocused on the road, his neighborhood a few streets away. "I'd rather demonstrate my learnings. Personally."

"Okay." I wasn't going to turn that offer down. "But only after another milkshake." I'd been craving one all day—something I never thought would happen after watching him make the first one. However, they'd become a part of my daily diet. Tray suspected it was a result of my fae side making up for lost time.

My powers were growing, too. I felt them simmering beneath the surface, my control a continued learning experience.

"Deal," Tray agreed, releasing my leg. "However, I require you to drink it naked. Consider it your *punishment*."

I snorted. "Sounds like something that'll punish you more than me, so sure."

His lips curled. "We'll see."

"Indeed we will."

Turned out, it was a punishment for us both.

One we thoroughly enjoyed.

CHAPTER TWENTY-TWO

ELLA

One Month Later

FRESHMAN ATTENDED THE Holiday Ball in December.

Seniors attended the Winter Ball in early February.

The similarities between the two made tonight perfect for what we had planned.

"Wow," Tray breathed from the doorway, his eyes roaming over my black gown and the slit running up my left leg to the middle of my thigh. It was one of the most risqué outfits I'd ever worn, hugging my figure in all the right places and dipping low into my cleavage.

It was the kind of dress a supermodel wore to a fancy gala or a celebrity event.

And it was perfect for tonight.

"You really are like a fairy guardian, Tray," I teased him, thinking of the conversation we had after Homecoming. Because once again, he'd chosen the gown, and this was my favorite one yet.

"Fuck fairies," he scoffed, sauntering into the room in a sinful black suit. "I'm all fae, baby." He wrapped his palm around the back of my neck, tugging me toward him for a long, sensual kiss.

"My fae," I murmured, smiling.

"Your fae," he agreed, angling his mouth over mine.

He tasted like fresh mint. I dipped my tongue inside, indulging myself in more as I clutched his shoulders. *Mmm, I could do this all night.*

Me, too, he agreed. *But we'll miss the dance.*

And what a shame that would be, I thought, unable to hold back my sarcasm.

"Mmm, we put too much into tonight to miss it now," he said, nipping my lower lip. "Ryan still thinks I intend to ruin you."

"I really don't know how you've managed to convince her that's still your plan with everything else that's occurred." Her reputation at the academy was soiled after her most recent erratic behavior—courtesy of my occasional taunting jolt.

Every time I felt bad for provoking her, I recalled all the horrible things she'd done to me over the years. The fact that she desperately wanted to ruin me tonight only fueled me onward. She needed a healthy dose of her own medicine. Maybe then she'd stop tormenting people.

And Carmen.

Oh, Carmen.

She wore a wig every day now and had already begun consultations for plastic surgery to fix some of the scarring—which wasn't even that bad. Unfortunately, her personality hadn't changed much, apart from adding a layer of whining to the mix.

So she hadn't really learned her lesson yet.

It was something I planned to revisit after our finale tonight.

"The compulsion these last few weeks helped," Tray admitted, pressing his forehead to mine.

"Yeah." I knew he'd woven some compulsion into his statements. After all the rumors started flying about her losing her mantle of queen, Tray had needed to do damage control. "I can't wait for all this to be done."

"Me, too," he whispered against my mouth.

We both agreed that graduating from high school really wasn't needed. Especially after what we'd discovered last week regarding my father's will. And, aside from that, a GED wouldn't mean much at Midnight Fae Academy. However, I still planned to apply for mine. My advanced curriculums and grades would allow me to qualify for early graduation. Not to mention, the administrative board wouldn't have a choice after Tray's plan came to fruition next week.

It all meant I would be free to move to the Midnight Fae Realm with Tray, where I could practice my magic freely.

Finally.

"Take me to the dance, Tray. Before I decide this isn't worth our time and demand you take me to bed instead."

He grinned. "Mmm, if you would just allow me to kill them all, it would go much faster." He phrased it as a joke, but I knew he meant it.

"This will be better."

"So you say." He linked his fingers through mine and tugged me toward the door. "I still say a bloody end would be more entertaining."

"Such a vampy thing to say."

"Midnight Fae, darling. Not vampires. Midnight. Fae." He gave me a look. "Did you not read that history text I gave you? It clearly explained what we are."

I rolled my eyes. "Yes, Professor Nacht. I remember."

"Headmaster Nacht," he corrected from the top of the stairs. "Or Prince Trayton. I'll accept either title from you in the bedroom, darling."

"Dead Nacht has a much better ring to it," I mused while following him downward toward the foyer. "Especially if you want me to call you either of those names *in the bedroom.*"

He chuckled and tugged me into a kiss near the front door, his lips holding a hint of dominance against mine. "I bet I could convince you otherwise."

"Maybe," I breathed, wrapping my palm around the back of his neck. I slid my tongue into his mouth, reveling in his taste once more, and pressed my body flush against his.

His growl of approval dampened the silk between my thighs. This man did such wicked things to me, and I adored him all the more for it. He wrapped an arm around my waist and clasped my jaw with his opposite hand. "Keep this up and we're never going to make it to the ball."

"Didn't you hire another limo?" I nibbled his jaw. "We could warm up in the backseat."

He groaned and yanked me outside. The chill in the air did nothing to dispel the heat between us. Tray all but carried me down the recently shoveled driveway to the waiting limousine parked on the street. Snow glistened all around us beneath the moon, painting the scene of a romantic night that I longed to enjoy at least for a little while.

And Tray willfully obliged.

He pulled me onto his lap in the backseat and wasted no time finding my mouth once more. His hands drifted up my sides to the straps of my gown, pulling them down my arms to expose my breasts.

"Fuck, I love this dress on you," he whispered, his lips trailing downward to my hardening peaks. He took one deep into his mouth, causing me to cry out and arch against him.

I barely noticed the limo rumbling to life.

Didn't even care if the driver heard me or knew what we were doing.

The way Tray seduced my body to heed his every desire left me winded and writhing on top of him. Having access to his mind only intensified the experience, hearing his wants and needs providing an intimate map for me to navigate. One I excelled at following, my sense of direction being a skill I'd worked tirelessly over the years to perfect.

He unbuttoned his dress pants. Slid down the zipper. And slipped my panties to the side to plunge inside me in a single thrust.

Oh, that slit on my dress certainly came in handy, making it far too easy for him to take me with all our clothes still intact. Which only seemed to make me burn hotter for him.

The silver cuff he gifted me stayed at home, leaving me free to play with my new talents. And I used them to caress him, the darkness pouring from me in a cloud that engulfed us both.

It urged him to move faster.

Harder.

To take me to new heights and beyond.

"You're killing me, Ella," he breathed, his pace increasing as he found my mouth once more.

Our pants and moans were all that followed, our minds and bodies fully attuned to each other.

It was always like this between us—passionate, consuming, and otherworldly. Most days, I couldn't believe this had become my life.

Others, I couldn't imagine it any other way.

I came around him on a groan, my soul and heart rejoicing as he followed me swiftly into oblivion. We never stopped kissing. Never stopped touching. Never stopped *existing*.

Even as I came down from the high, all I wanted was more.

Unfortunately, that wouldn't be possible until after the dance.

Until after we finished this once and for all.

I kissed him soundly, pouring all my emotions into his

mouth with my tongue, and he returned the favor in kind before eventually helping me fix my dress. His clever use of the handkerchief from his breast pocket had me giggling. "So that's the point of those—to help clean up."

He smirked. "Well, it's one use."

We never used a condom between us because diseases weren't an issue for the fae, and pregnancy apparently was controlled by the male.

I had some choice opinions on that part, but Tray assured me he would never trigger it without talking to me first. As I could read his mind, I knew he meant it.

He pressed his lips to my temple. "Ready, Ella?"

I nodded, relaxing into his side. "Yes."

Tonight marked the end of an era.

And the beginning of a new one.

CHAPTER TWENTY-THREE

✿ ELLA ✿

THE WINTER BALL WAS HELD in the same venue as the Holiday Ball, making the surroundings eerily familiar. Only, the decorations were blue and silver, not red and green. But everything else reminded me of that fated night from years ago.

Including the *prince* standing near the staircase. I had to begrudgingly admit that Dash had aged well, his handsome face slightly more cut and edged than his freshman version. He was also about six inches taller with broader shoulders. But I recognized the dick beneath the exterior, that same arrogant flare radiating from his too-blue eyes as he grinned at everyone who approached him.

My stomach tightened as he met my gaze.

I had a mission tonight that included him, and this was

exactly what I needed to have happen, but, ugh, I so did not want to do this. But I forced my lips to curl into a shy smile—as I'd done for the last few weeks while I'd pretended to tolerate his presence.

He canted his head to the side in unspoken invitation, and I nodded.

It meant he wanted to talk, something he'd done twice to me over the last month. However, it'd always been about immaterial shit. Like the weather or class assignments. Such a weird thing for us to discuss after years of endless bickering.

Although, really, most of that bickering had been instigated by Charlie. It sort of left Dash and me without a means of communication. As though we didn't know how to converse now that we weren't fighting.

Which both negatively and positively impacted my plan of attack.

He wants to talk, I told Tray as I took a step forward. Tray had purposely left me alone on this side of the room, knowing Dash would take the opportunity to grab my attention. Our entire scheme hinged on the assumption that Dash was attracted to me—something I still didn't believe. But I'd play along for now and see if I couldn't find a way to trap him.

I see that, Tray replied softly. *If he touches you, I won't be able to stop myself from intervening.*

It took effort not to roll my eyes. *I can handle myself.* Dash didn't frighten me so much as repulse me.

Yes, I'm aware, love. It's me who will have trouble controlling myself in this scenario.

Yet, this was all your idea, I reminded him in a singsong voice.

No, I wanted to kill him. You told me to think of alternatives, and this was a suggestion—one I regret right now.

It'll be fine, I promised, stopping in front of Dash. "Hi."

"Hey," he replied, his trademark cocky air missing from that single word. "Can we, uh, talk somewhere?" His tone and demeanor were a stark contrast to his approach at Homecoming where he demanded a dance.

I nearly frowned. It couldn't be this easy, could it? *I think he's up to something.*

Same, Tray agreed. *Be careful.*

I left my cuff at home, I thought back at him, smiling inside. Dash would severely regret it if he tried something. "Sure," I said, giving him a tight smile. "Lead the way."

He nodded, his posture oddly uneasy.

Yeah, he's definitely up to something, I decided.

Tray remained quiet, but I felt his protective energy swimming around me in a comforting caress.

Neither of us had seen Ryan yet, which was odd since Dash was her date for the ball. Maybe that was where he led me now—to an ambush orchestrated by her. I wouldn't be surprised.

But when we came to a stop in a well-lit corridor with no waiting attackers, I frowned. "What are we doing, Dash?" I finally asked, deciding there was no point in drawing this out.

"Talking," he replied, turning to face me with an expression unlike any I'd ever seen from him. He almost appeared... sad. Contrite, even. He palmed the back of his neck and blew out a breath. "Look. I owe you an apology." He winced and shook his head. "Several, really."

"Okay..." *I think he's about to confess something.*

Good. The camera is already on, Tray reminded me.

Right.

The one in the tiara on my head. Tray had affixed it to my hair before we left the limo. It had a camera custombuilt into one of the prongs. Where he found it, or how it was created, I had no idea. The man possessed a lot of skills that impressed me, this being one of them.

Dash cleared his throat and glanced up at the ceiling. "Fuck, I don't even know where to start. I didn't pick up Ryan tonight, despite her edicts to the contrary. She's going to be livid when she finally gets here, and I'm sure I'll be bearing the brunt of that anger. So I almost stayed home, but I couldn't just sit by knowing what's going to happen tonight. I had to tell you. To warn you."

Yeah, this wasn't at all where I expected this conversation to go. "Warn me about what, Dash?" And he left Ryan at home? Wow. I wished I could have been there to see her face when she realized he wasn't coming.

"I'm sorry, Ella. You have no idea how many times I've wanted to say that to you over the years. I was such a dick to you at the Holiday Ball. No excuse in the world can justify my behavior, so I won't even try. But not a day goes by that I don't regret my actions."

My brow furrowed. "So why did you do it?" This was the part I wanted him to admit, the piece of information I needed to play before the school.

"Does it matter?" he asked, his tone holding a touch of derision. "We both know Ryan and Carmen put me up to it, but that's just an excuse. As is admitting that I was a stupid kid who fell beneath the manipulation of two world-class bitches."

There, I thought, triumphant. *He admitted it.*

But he wasn't done.

"I loathe them, Ella. And I hate even more who I am when I'm with them." He released the back of his neck and stuffed his hands into his pockets, his posture that of a scared boy rather than the intimidating male he usually put on for the school.

"These last few months have been... enlightening." He cleared his throat. "You've stood up to them—to all of us— for years. But you've taken it to a whole new level, your confidence sky-high."

I had no idea how to reply to that. So I went with, "Uh... 'kay. Thanks?"

He laughed nervously and shook his head. "I'm fucking this up. What I'm trying to tell you is, I'm an idiot. Homecoming was actually the major turning point for me because of the way I felt after you ran away—*again*. The first time, I'd been a stupid kid. However, this time, well, I honestly couldn't believe the things that had come out of my mouth or how I'd grabbed you. I realized in that moment that I wasn't the man I want to be at all. But a fucking dick."

Okay, yeah, this definitely wasn't where I expected this conversation to go at all.

The surprise radiating from my mating bond said Tray felt the same. He expected Dash to make a move, to apologize for his behavior as a way of getting into my pants. But he didn't seem to be heading in that direction at all. If anything, I felt like a priest in a confessional booth listening to this boy expel all his sins.

"Anyway, I know Tray is part of the reason you've changed lately, which is why I'm here tonight," Dash continued. "It would have been so much easier to just stay home, let Ryan stew, and just blow her off Monday. But after everything I've put you through, I couldn't just sit by and let her ruin you all over again. Because what she's planning? It can destroy a person. And you don't deserve that, Ella. Fuck, you don't deserve *any* of this shit."

"What are you trying to tell me, Dash?" I demanded, my stomach twisting painfully. "What is she planning?"

"She's gone on and on about it for months." He glanced upward, sideways, anywhere but at me. "It's like she *lives* to hurt you."

"Not telling me what I want to know," I said, my patience waning by the second. Because yeah, I was very aware of my stepsister's hatred and penchant for causing me harm. "Spit it out, Dash."

He flinched, those piercing eyes meeting mine. "She's made sure you'll be crowned Winter Queen tonight with Tray as the Winter King. And then he's going to announce to everyone how it was all a game to win your virginity. That none of it was real. He's been playing you from the beginning, Ella."

My shoulders sagged in relief. "Oh, that." Fuck, for a

moment I thought she had another plan up her sleeve that I hadn't anticipated. This one, I could handle.

Dash's lips curled downward, then his eyes widened. "You already knew."

"Of course she did," Tray said, joining us in the hallway.

I'd felt him creeping closer as a result of my unease, ready to kick the shit out of Dash on a second's notice. So when he wrapped his arm around me, I melted into him on a contented sigh. "Yeah, I knew. He told me after Homecoming."

Tray kissed my temple and held me closer. "I have no intention of following Ryan's orders tonight. Because, unlike you, I'm not afraid of that cunt or her meager threats. She can kiss my ass."

Dash ran his fingers through his hair, his posture still one of defeat and so unlike the Dash Charming I'd known for years. "I'm glad you're here," he said after a beat. "And that you met Ella. She deserves someone like you."

"Wrong, she deserves someone better than me. But I'm lucky she puts up with me anyway."

I rolled my eyes and nudged him with my elbow. "Whatever, Nacht. I barely tolerate you."

He chuckled, his amusement heating our bond. "Just barely."

"It's true," I said with a shrug.

Dash stood grinning at us. "I should have known you weren't playing into Ryan's game, but you had me convinced otherwise. Man, she's going to be livid when she realizes you fucked her over."

"Like I care," Tray drawled. "As I said, she doesn't scare me."

"I can see that." Dash cleared his throat and erected his spine. "Well, anyway, I'm glad you're here. And, Ella, I'm sorry. I know that means shit in the grand scheme of things, that I owe you a hell of a lot more than a measly apology, but all I can do is try."

"Which is why you told her about Ryan's plans tonight,"

Tray added.

Dash nodded. "I didn't..." He swallowed, grimacing. "I didn't want to see that night repeated. And I knew this would be much worse because she never looked at me the way she looks at you. The kind of destruction Ryan is, or was, planning... it's the kind of thing that really fucks someone up."

He let that sit between the three of us.

The soft beat of the ballroom vibrated beneath my heels, the rhythm matching the subdued one of my pulse.

"Charlie's leaving has softened you," Tray finally said.

Dash lifted a shoulder. "I don't know about softened, but it's forced me to put a few things into perspective. That guy was a real dick."

"So are you," Tray pointed out.

"I am," he agreed. "But I'm working on fixing that."

Three months ago, I'd have called bullshit. But I couldn't deny his behavior had changed since Charlie left. And the way he'd come to me tonight? That suggested sincerity in his actions.

I don't think we can show this to the school, I told Tray, swallowing.

That'd been our original plan—we'd make him confess that Ryan encouraged him to torment me, then put him and Ryan on blast together. While he still technically deserved it, I didn't see the point in punishing a guy who was clearly already punishing himself and trying to change at the same time.

I know, he whispered back to me. *I turned off the feed before joining you in the hall.*

"Well..." Dash cleared his throat again. "I'll, uh, let you two enjoy the rest of your night."

He took a step, but Tray moved into his path. "Just so we're clear, the only reason I've not kicked your ass for hurting Ella is because I know she wouldn't approve. I also didn't want to take the opportunity away from her, should she want to beat you the way you deserve. But if you breathe a word of any of this to Ryan before we have a chance to finish this game, I will destroy you in ways you can't even imagine."

Power radiated from my mate. Dash wouldn't see it, but I had no doubt he could *feel* it. And the widening of his eyes confirmed my suspicion. "I don't know what you have planned for Ryan, but I won't stand in your way. And I won't breathe a word of any of this to her."

"See that you don't," Tray murmured, his voice low and lethal. "Because I'll know if you do. And you will regret it." He allowed that threat to linger between them before returning to my side. "Continue on your path, Charming. It's the right one."

That almost sounded like a prophecy, but I knew from talking to Tray that Midnight Fae weren't seers. However, apparently that kind of fae did exist—the Fortune Fae.

I shivered as Tray circled my waist with his arm.

We watched as Dash left, his shoulders caving yet again. It was so strange to see him appear weak after ruling the academy for so long. "Do you think he's truly going to change?" I wondered out loud.

"I think he's already changing," Tray said, holding me close. "It's not how I anticipated things to evolve after removing Charlie from the equation, but I can't say I'm disappointed by it."

"Neither am I," I admitted. "But I don't think the others are going to be so easy."

He snorted. "No, your wicked witch of a stepsister doesn't have a heart. It's why I still vote for burning her alive."

I shook my head, grinning. "You really want to kill her."

"It's a fantasy I'd love to see come true."

"How about a public roast instead?" I suggested.

He glanced down at me. "I thought you just said I can't kill her? But yes, roasting her is something I'd enjoy observing."

"I'm talking about the act of ridiculing, not a fire,

Nacht." Sometimes our backgrounds crossed and I had to play fae interpreter for the human language.

Disappointment flashed in his features. "And here I thought there'd be bloodshed tonight."

"Well, that remains to be seen." It all depended on how this went down.

Right on cue, an announcement sounded from the ballroom, giving the Royal Court a thirty-minute warning for the festivities.

Ryan might be pissed about Dash standing her up, but she wouldn't miss this for the world.

Which meant she'd be here soon.

"Let's get this party started," I mused, taking Tray's hand.

"No, baby." He threaded his fingers through mine. "We're not starting anything. We're finishing it."

CHAPTER TWENTY-FOUR

TRAY

OH, RYAN WAS PISSED.

Everyone gave her a wide berth as she marched toward Dash with steam practically billowing from her ears. She grabbed his arm and yanked him away from the group of females he'd been chatting up, her ire hitting a boiling point. "What. The. Fuck?"

He twisted out of her grip and took a step back from her. "I believe that's my line, Ryan. What makes you think you can touch me like that?"

"Oh, I don't know. Maybe the fact that you're *my date* and you failed to pick me up and take me to dinner, making me wait several hours just to find you here with these floozies instead?"

"I never agreed to be your date," he replied coolly. "You

made assumptions, and that's not my problem." He made to turn away from her, but a screech from her had him cocking a brow. "What now, Ryan?"

"How *dare* you stand me up!"

"Stand you up?" He laughed. "We don't belong to each other, remember? You made that very clear three years ago." He gave her a condescending smile. "If you've changed your mind, I'm sorry, but it's too late. I haven't been interested in you in quite some time."

Her mouth actually fell open, her usual spitfire retorts lost to the chatter growing around them.

Well, that's a fun twist in our evening plans, Ella mused beside me, her lips curling. *He's just publicly shamed her for us.*

Oh, and that's just an appetizer, darling. I had a speech planned that would demolish Ryan's reputation.

Ella liked the symbolism of me being the one to speak tonight since it'd been Dash all those years ago who'd announced his true intentions to the school. It only seemed appropriate that I do the same tonight in a similar manner, but with very different words.

The music lowered to a dull background sound as two of Darlington Academy's administrators ascended the stage. *Were they present at the Holiday Ball?* I asked, an idea forming in my head.

Yep. Ella narrowed her eyes at them. *They always look the other way. That night was no different.*

Oh, they'll be taking notice tonight, I promised.

Ella knew what I'd done, even if I never admitted it out loud. Her access to my mind made it impossible to hide things from her. I'd sensed her acceptance of it the moment she learned my intentions, her thoughts almost always in tune with mine.

It was why we made a good team.

I can't wait to hear your acceptance speech, she purred at me, leading me toward the stage with her hand locked in mine.

When we reached the platform, I grabbed her and kissed her hard on the mouth. When I pulled back, Ryan gave me a knowing look. As though she thought I'd only done that to say goodbye.

I winked at her, allowing her to think whatever she liked, and wrapped my arm around Ella's shoulders. Meanwhile, Dash positioned himself away from Ryan on the opposite side of the stage. He leveled me with a warning look, one that dared me to misstep.

It further confirmed his feelings for Ella. I thought he was just attracted to her, but after the display in the hall, the way he tried to protect her, I suspected they ran deeper. The way he challenged me now drove that point home.

You had your chance with her, I told him with my eyes. *She's mine now.*

Not that he ever posed any real competition.

Ella was fated to be mine from birth. Our souls confirmed it when we bonded, and that connection between us was unbreakable.

She leaned into me, her gaze sparkling. *Even if you're right about his feelings, I'll never return them.*

I know.

Then stop trying to murder him with your eyes. She went to her tippy-toes to brush a kiss over my mouth. *I trust you, Trayton Nacht. Now destroy my stepsister, please. I want to go home.*

My lips twitched. I almost asked if that meant I could light the bitch on fire, but the ceremony began with crowning the Winter King and Winter Queen.

I really didn't understand the human obsession with these sorts of titles, but I supposed living in a real royal family skewed my view a bit.

Ella received her crown first and did an excellent job of acting shocked and dismayed, while in her mind she ridiculed the stupid tradition. "As I already have a tiara," she said, glancing at me, "I'll just hold this for now until Tray can help me fix my hair."

"You were already a princess to me, darling," I replied, loud enough for everyone to hear.

Ryan snorted.

Other people sighed.

The administrators smiled.

Ella returned to my side, her excitement contagious. Her thoughts were underlined with a hint of nerves, reminiscent of past hurts, but she followed each concern with a justification.

Tray won't hurt me. He's my mate. This will be fine. Ryan's going down.

I didn't reply, preparing myself for the speech I was about to make.

When the administrators called my name, announcing me as Winter King, I glanced at them and ignored their silly crown. It was a cheap plastic knockoff very unlike the tiara I'd placed on Ella earlier tonight. She didn't know—because I'd hidden it from her—but it was actually a family heirloom interlaced with fae magic.

Her eyes widened as I revealed that to her in my thoughts.

You're a princess now, I reminded her. *Never forget it.*

Fairy Guardian, she returned, causing my lips to twitch as I took the microphone.

"Wow. Winter King." I pretended to ponder that for a moment. "I can't imagine a more ridiculous title, to be honest. Why the hell would I want to be Winter King of this dreadful place?" My focus shifted to the shocked administrators. "I mean, the things you all allow to happen here is just mind-blowing. Allow me to demonstrate."

I removed the microphone from the stand before they could take it from me and stepped to the side so I could see both Ella and Ryan.

The latter grinned triumphantly.

Ella, however, held a regal stance that would make my mother—and likely hers as well—proud.

"You know, babe"—I purposely picked a nickname I never used for Ella—"it's been an interesting few months. All these games." I shook my head. "I mean, honestly, I'm shocked you fell for it all. You actually think I'd want you?

When I can have her?"

Ella flinched, even though I wasn't talking to her but to Ryan. The words were just too reminiscent of Dash's speech all those years ago, as I assumed the resulting gasps from the crowd were, too.

"While you've been ensnared in my web, I've carefully dismantled every facet of your life. All for the promise of bedding you, which is something I never wanted to do."

"Mr. Nacht," a feminine voice interjected. Professor Montgomery stood on the side of the stage, her expression livid. "Give me that microphone right now."

"No, I'm not done." And there was no way she'd be able to take this from me now. "And while I appreciate you finally growing a conscience and truly standing up for your student, you're about three years too late. Because let's be honest, all your previous attempts haven't been all that successful." She was also protecting the wrong girl.

Ryan chuckled, the sound vile and cruel. "Keep going," she encouraged.

"Oh, I intend to." I smiled brilliantly at her. "When you approached me about seducing your stepsister and asking me to break her heart publicly, I couldn't have been happier. Because you single-handedly gave me the power to destroy you instead."

A pin could have dropped at that pronouncement.

And Ryan's mouth fell open.

Way to dive right in, Ella said into my mind.

No time like the present, I returned.

"You know, I wondered how someone could be so vicious as to offer herself… Oh, wait, no. You promised me a threesome between you and Carmen, right? Yeah, hard pass, sweetheart. Ella satisfies me in ways neither of you could ever begin to comprehend. But back to what I was saying—I tried to figure out how someone could be so cruel to another person, let alone a family member." I reached into my pocket to pull out my phone. "However, after some digging with Ella, we figured it out."

My eyes wandered to my mate, searching her features and mind for any kind of distress and finding her perfectly at ease.

So I continued.

"In case it's not obvious by now—as I know some of you may need these things spelled out for you—Ryan hired me to fuck Ella and dump her in front of the school. Sort of like what happened a few years ago at the Holiday Ball, only worse since my task was to capture her heart. Which I believe I've done." I cocked a brow at my mate.

She merely smiled, the look coy and secretive.

Devious minx, I accused playfully.

Delectable fairy, she replied.

I nearly sighed out loud. *That whole punishment thing lingers in your future, El.*

Bring it on, Nacht.

I smirked. "Yes, for those wondering, Ella's been aware of her stepsister's intentions for a while now," I said, holding her gaze and ignoring all the whispers coming from the room, as well as Ryan's resulting growl.

But movement across the stage had me sending a sliver of magic to ground the administrators, who had begun to shuffle toward me. They'd attribute the sensation to having their limbs locked in shock.

In reality, I'd frozen them.

Because I wasn't done.

"Ah, here it is." I made a show of looking at my phone and pulled up the will Ella and I had uncovered recently. Then I cleared my throat to begin reading. After it became obvious what I held in my palm, I paused and looked at Ryan. "Really, there's a bunch of legal bullshit that I don't want to bore the audience with. So let's jump to the important part where Tremaine Cinder—Ella's father, for those of you not paying attention—declared Isabella Cinder as his sole heir to his fortune. Clarissa Cinder is listed as the legal guardian of the estate, but only effective until Isabella's eighteenth birthday. Which was when, darling?"

"Roughly five months ago," she confirmed.

"Yes, which means you own everything." I feigned shock as I refocused at a fuming Ryan. "Surely you didn't know?" Then I smiled, dropping the act. "Except we all know you did. And you've been trying to beat Ella into submission all these years since learning the truth—that you'd be *nothing* without your gorgeous, intelligent, cunning stepsister."

I faced the administrators, adding, "It also means all those checks you've been cashing from Clarissa Cinder these last few months—the ones that allow her children to terrorize the halls—were never hers to write."

Ella smiled. *Mic drop.*

I smirked. *Indeed.* That was a human phrase I enjoyed. Although, I was tempted to literally release the microphone. It would make for a lovely sound that would startle the room from their stupor.

"So, Ryan, you're living in a home you have no rights to, driving a car that isn't yours, and attending an academy that you could never afford without Ella's permission. How fascinating that you decided to involve me in your little family drama. All for what? The promise of one night with you. Which brings me back to—how the fuck could you ever think I'd choose you over Isabella?" I looked her over in obvious distaste. "Not even if you paid me, babe."

"I think that's enough, Mr. Nacht," Professor Montgomery tried again.

"I don't agree, Peggy," I drawled. "Because, you see, the academy is about to fall under new management. When I told Father how poorly this place is run and the shenanigans allowed in these halls, he put some measures in place—and by that, I mean new ownership." This was the part I hadn't outwardly discussed with Ella, but she knew about it through our bond. And while she felt it was a waste of resources, she agreed with my thought process.

Because owning the academy ensured that nothing like this could ever happen again.

It also allowed us to secure her early graduation, something her mother's inheritance required. Not that Ella really needed the funds after the hefty amount her father had left for her, but it was the principle of the matter at this point. Besides, she deserved her degree after all the shit she'd put up with over the last three and a half years. And I would ensure that she received it without having to set another foot inside that awful place.

Of course, it was about to change drastically.

"I believe the majority of you will be dismissed on Monday," I added, grinning. "I suggest you work on those resumes tomorrow." With a contented sigh, I smiled at my mate. "Have I missed anything, darling?"

"No, I think that about wraps it up. Can we go—"

Ryan's palm nearly connected with Ella's face, but my mate caught her stepsister's wrist before she could finish the movement.

And sent the bitch backward several feet with a shock I felt through the bond.

The scream splitting Ryan's lips made even me cringe.

Ella had zapped her hard.

But to the room, it looked like she'd shoved Ryan. At least, that was what their minds would interpret. Anything else would be too difficult for a mortal mind to believe.

"Do not fucking touch me," Ella snapped, her voice carrying across the hushed room. "Your reign over my life ended months ago, Ryan. However, mine over yours is just beginning. Because I will be taking back the house and all the assets your mother has stolen from me."

She stepped forward to stare down at the now cowering female on the floor.

"But don't worry, *sis*," Ella continued. "I'll be providing you all with an allowance to live on. It'll be just enough to keep you off the streets until you graduate from public school. Then you can go work and make your own money."

She held out her hand for mine. "I'm ready to go now."

I read between the lines.

She didn't mean back to my home here in Darlington but to the one in the Midnight Fae Realm.

To where we both belonged.

I laced my fingers with hers and used my other hand to return the microphone. "Oh, I'm done," I said to the room, smiling. "Enjoy your Winter Ball."

The shock of the room followed us all the way to the door.

As we left without once looking back.

We were done with the present and moving firmly into the future to create our own happily ever after.

Together.

EPILOGUE

Three and a Half Years Later

"UGH, your mother is killing me with these gowns." Every time we spent the summer with his parents, she insisted on dressing me up like a little doll. The woman considered me the daughter she never had, and since Kols refused to accept his mate, I was alone in my torment.

Not that Kols's mate, Emelyn, would make it any better.

Hell, that bitch would make this worse.

So yeah, I'd choose this fate over her as a sister-in-law any day. She'd put Ryan to shame.

"Oh, I don't know," Tray drawled, overhearing my thoughts. "I think they'd pair well locked in a closet. We could add Carmen in for fun, give them all some knives, and watch the bloodshed."

"For once, I might be on board with your lethal idea." While I'd essentially taken everything from Ryan and Carmen, they'd yet to acquire an ounce of humanity.

The only good thing that came of it was that they held little influence over others, leaving them to drive each other—and Clarissa—mad. It seemed the general public was safe from them. For now. But I'd continue to watch, and now that I'd mastered most of my talents, I'd use them as needed to keep those bitches in line.

Fortunately, Dash had grown into a rather pleasant guy, his studies at Harvard going well while he held on to a steady girlfriend of over a year now. We didn't keep in touch, but Tray had kept up with him, prepared to intervene if necessary. But it seemed he'd meant it when he claimed to want to change.

And Charlie, well, he was obsolete now that Anderson Motors filed for bankruptcy.

No one had heard from him in over a year.

And I didn't care enough to look for him.

Tray caught the zipper at my back to help me out of my dress and kissed my nape. "We'll be returning to the Academy soon, dove," he whispered, replying to my complaint about all the gowns.

"Where I'll be stuck in uniforms," I drawled, glancing at him over my shoulder. He'd failed to mention that little requirement when telling me about the Academy. It seemed my entire life would be about wearing the same clothes as everyone else.

He smirked. "One more year. Then we're done."

The thought of being finished with our studies improved my mood immensely. While I still didn't know where I fit into this world, I was excited to learn my place with Tray by my side. He would join the Council because of his birthright, serving as a second-in-command to his brother—the future king.

Which reminded me... "How was the meeting?" He'd

just returned from some sort of urgent discussion. His annoyance flickered through our bond, causing my eyebrows to sail upward. "That bad, huh?"

Tray helped me out of my dress and handed me one of his shirts—which was my chosen sleep attire. "Yeah. It's bad."

He pulled off his tie and started unbuttoning his dress shirt before switching to his cuff links. I slid under the sheets as he removed his jacket, and waited for him to take off the rest of his clothes.

Warily, he joined me in just his boxers, his shoulders sagging on a sigh. "Shade bit an Elemental Fae."

My eyes widened. "*What?*" I knew a little about their kind. They were divided into sects based on their affinity for earth, air, water, fire, or spirit. And they didn't need human blood to survive.

"Yeah. And she's not just any Elemental Fae, but a Royal Earth Fae," Tray said, running his fingers through his thick hair. "My father is livid."

"Of course he is." It was illegal to mate outside of our race. My being a Halfling was the only exception. "What are they going to do?"

"They're sending her to the Academy." He glanced at me, and I knew I wasn't going to like whatever he said next. "And they've assigned her to our suite on Elite Quad. Specifically, they want you to share a room with her."

I blinked. "What? Why?"

"To keep an eye on her until they figure out how to handle the situation," he muttered. "Look, I'm not thrilled about it, but I prefer it to killing her. Which was the other option on the table."

"Kill a royal?"

"They're afraid of how Shade's bite will influence her powers." He collapsed beside me on the bed, shaking his head. "That fucking prick. And of course, they're letting him remain at the Academy, too. He's under strict orders not to bite her again, but we both know that's not going to stop him."

"Have they lost their minds? He should be locked up for doing that to her."

"They're giving him the benefit of the doubt for reporting the crime." Tray's expression told me how he felt about that. "I suspect he did it on purpose."

"Why? Why would he do that?"

"Your guess is as good as mine." He blew out a breath. "So I suppose our final year is going to be an interesting one. They're moving her to the Academy tonight."

I frowned. "But classes don't start for another week."

"Headmaster Zeph is in charge of introducing her to the grounds and helping her settle." His dark eyes locked on mine. "Gives us six or seven days to prepare for our inevitable introduction."

"And I'm supposed to live with her?"

"You're the only female in our suite," he explained. "And my dad was pretty clear about her staying near me and Kols for protection." He lifted onto his elbow and palmed my cheek. "We'll figure it out, El. The Council just wants us to help her acclimate. That's all."

"What if she doesn't want to *acclimate*?" I asked, arching a brow.

"Then it'll be a good thing she has you." He waggled his brows. "I've never met a stronger, more stubborn female in my life. You'll be her greatest ally within days. I'm sure of it."

I snorted. "Or we'll kill each other." I didn't get along with many of the fae on campus, which wasn't surprising considering I grew up without friends. A few of them were okay. Most I avoided because they were either jealous of my mating to Tray or had an issue with my Halfling status. "I suppose we'll have our rare histories in common."

What with me being the only one of my kind on campus and her being from another realm entirely.

"That's the spirit, love," he murmured, nudging me onto my back and sliding a thigh between my legs. "Now I suggest we spend the next few days losing ourselves in the sheets, as we might not have as many opportunities once we return."

I narrowed my eyes up at him. "Uh-huh. Because having other people in our suite has stopped us before."

"Hey, this is a whole new entity. Who knows how this will impact our sex life?" He nuzzled my neck.

"I think you're just looking for excuses to fool around."

"I never need an excuse to fool around with you, El," he whispered against my throat. "Or to bite you. Or to love you. Or to kiss you." He trailed his lips up to my ear. "Or to fuck you." His words caused me to arch into him, my body already primed just from his return.

Nearly three years of knowing him and he still enticed me with a mere look. If anything, my attraction to him had only grown over time.

My arms wound around his neck, holding him. "Make love to me, Tray," I murmured. "Slow and meaningful. At least the first time." The second could be as rough or intense as he wanted. But for now, I was in the mood to feel our connection, to know how much we loved each other.

"It would be my pleasure, mate," he said, his mouth capturing mine.

I love you, I breathed into his mind.

I love you, too, El.

And he did.

Over and over again.

Until I fell into a deep sleep, wrapped up in his arms, with our entire future ahead of us. And as I dreamt, the name *Aflora* echoed throughout my mind.

Something dark was on the horizon.

I felt it in my bones, in the way my soul quivered.

Change is coming.

See you soon.

THIS IS THE END OF TRAY AND ELLA'S STORY,
BUT YOU'LL SEE THEM AGAIN IN THE *MIDNIGHT
FAE ACADEMY* TRILOGY...

Welcome to Midnight Fae Academy.
Home of the dark arts.
Vampires.
And cruelly handsome fae.

A forbidden bite led to my capture and recruitment.
There are no flowers here.
No life.
Only death.

I'm an Earth Fae who doesn't belong here.
They can play their little mind games all they want, but I'm going
to find a way back to my elemental world. Even if it kills me.

Except Headmaster Zephyrus is one step ahead of my every
move.
Prince Kolstov won't stop cornering me.
And Shadow—the reason I'm in this damn mess to begin
with—haunts my dreams.

My affinity for the earth is dying and being replaced by
something more sinister. Something powerful. Something
deadly.

The Midnight Fae believe this is my fate.
They claim that I was "recruited" for a purpose.
To battle a rising presence.
Or to die trying.

I don't owe them a damn thing. But if I have to pass their trials to find my way home, then so be it. I survived a plague and far worse in the Elemental Fae realm. An ominous energy? Please. What a joke.

Give it your best shot.
I'm waiting.
And don't you dare bite me.
Or I'll make you regret it.

Author Note: This is a dark paranormal reverse harem trilogy with bully romance (enemies-to-lovers) elements. Despite Aflora's opinions on the matter, there will definitely be biting. Shadow, aka Shade, guarantees it. This book ends on a cliffhanger.

ABOUT LEXI C. FOSS

USA Today Bestselling Author Lexi C. Foss loves to play in dark worlds, especially the ones that bite. She lives in Atlanta, Georgia with her husband and their furry children. When not writing, she's busy crossing items off her travel bucket list, or chasing eclipses around the globe. She's quirky, consumes way too much coffee, and loves to swim.

www.LexiCFoss.com
https://www.facebook.com/LexiCFoss
https://www.twitter.com/LexiCFoss

Printed in Great Britain
by Amazon